HEIR OF BLOOD AND GOLD
FABLES OF TARLATAN

SAMANTHA DEPERGOLA

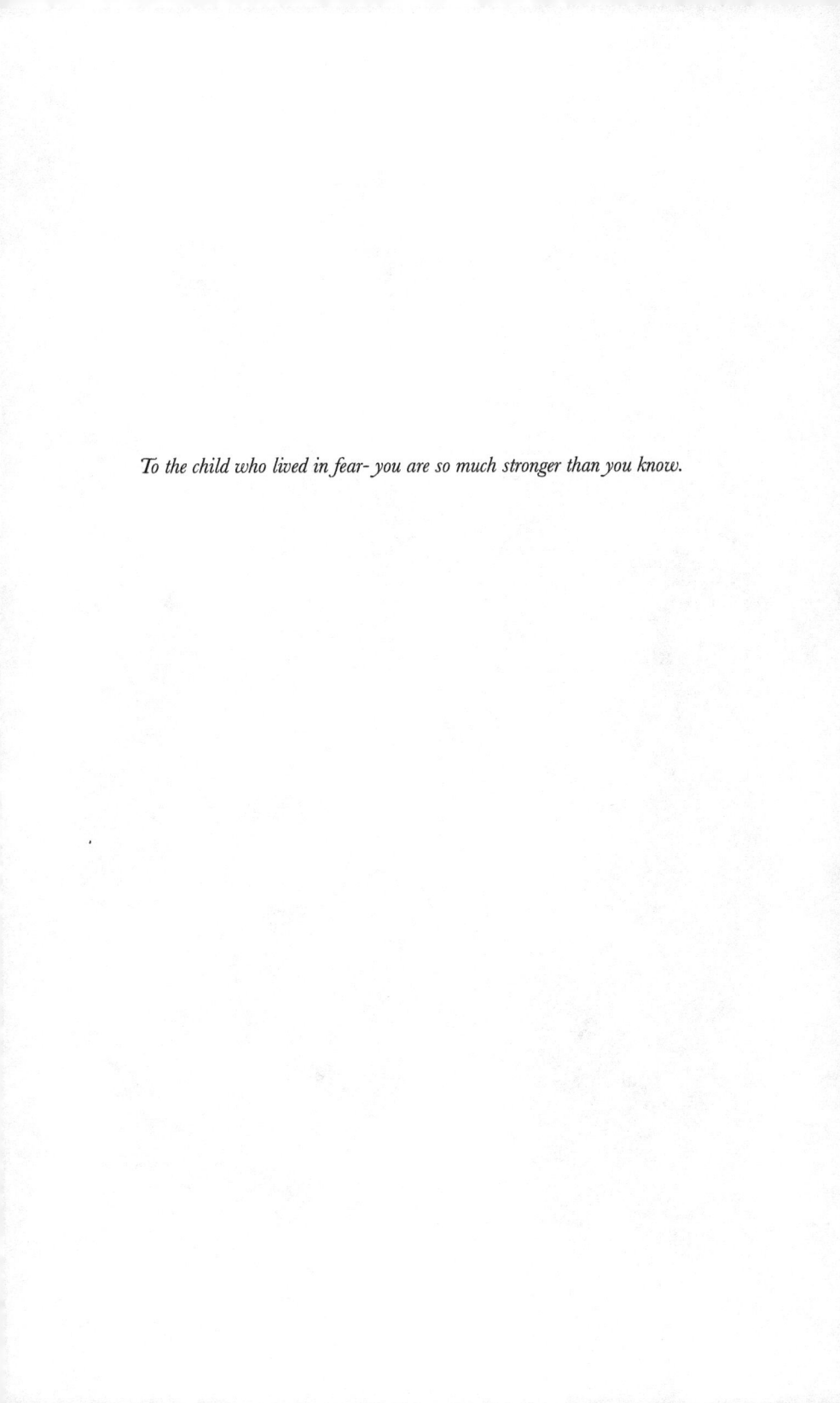

To the child who lived in fear- you are so much stronger than you know.

Tarlatan

West to the
Magicless

Charford

Nazare

Trefillon

Home of Thornmere

Luce Stellarum

Gru

Statium

Corsair

Lubeck

Rubicon

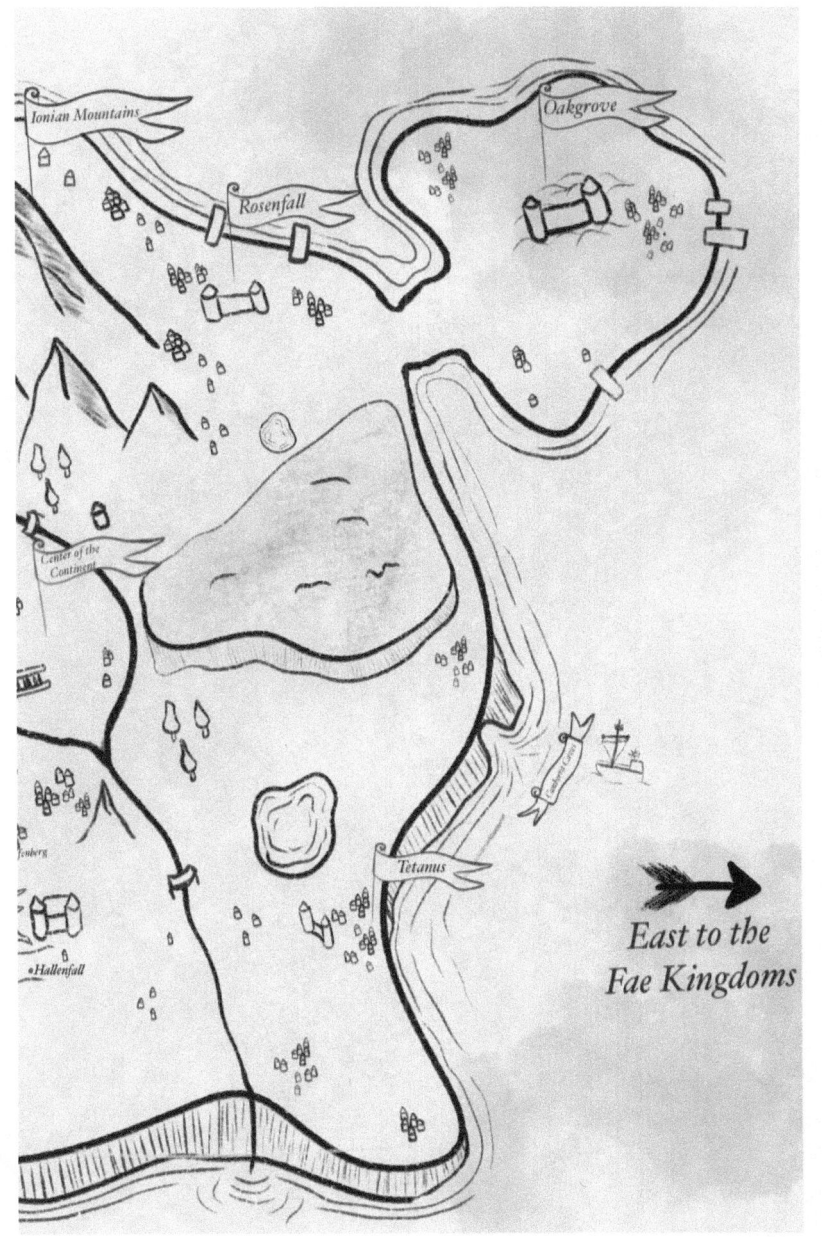

Ionian Mountains

Rosenfall

Oakgrove

Center of the
Continent

Tetanus

East to the
Fae Kingdoms

Hallenfall

CHAPTER 1

UNTANGLING THE THREADS
OF A STORY

The weary traveling group clip clopped into town, thankful they had horses. They had been adventuring for... Years, now, and couldn't imagine walking all over Tarlatan.

Jonathon looked at the small town, Clearford, seemingly sleeping in the distance. It had been so very long since he had been here and there was so much that had changed since then. Only the group leader, Jethro, understood the importance of the town to Jonathon. It was where Jonathon had decided where his destiny would lie.

Clearford was another coastal city north of Trifillem. It was slightly smaller than Trifillem, but no less bustling. From afar, the cottages that composed the outer ring of the town hid the market from view. To any traveler, Clearford was a sleepy town where there was little money to be made. But once you entered that inner ring...

The market was bustling with life, children running throughout the streets. Inns and taverns lined the streets with shops dotted throughout. Market stalls peppered the paths of taverns who offered them protection. Fish and furs were the prime seller at the market, with no better found until you hit Rosenfall.

The group behind him laughed at some obscure joke one of them had picked up from another town in the south of the continent. Jonathon smiled, but it didn't meet his eyes. Jethro tugged his horse closer to him, matching his pace.

"This is where you found me." Jonathon whispered. He noticed Jethro smiling next to him, his grey eyes nearly matching his greying hair. Jonathon had known this man for almost thirty years and still... He saw that man with his brown hair and muscled skin even when his muscles faded and hair lightened.

Jethro took a swig from his waterskin. "And I had to pay a hefty fee to release you from your apprenticeship. But you were worth it- every last bit of gold. The guild wouldn't be the same without you."

They continued on in silence for the rest of their journey as the hot sun rose and faded overhead. The days were growing short in Tarlatan as summer turned into fall.

And as the seasons turned... Something was brewing. Something that kept the bond between Jonathon and Thermaxas strung taught at all times.

The guild strode into town and slowed the horses further.

"Jonathon, watch the horses. We'll tie them up over here and I'll go inside to try to get us some rooms for the next few nights. Selma, can you go with the Jyn and Namior to get some supplies?" Jethro hopped off his horse, pulling Jonathon out of his reverie. A wince appeared on Jethro's face that Jonathon pretended not to notice. He pointed at the railing above a water trough and then the tavern across the road. Jonathon nodded, getting off as well and feeling his bones ache in protest.

Every time they stopped, it seemed like it got more difficult for all of them. The constant riding, sleeping in camps, and lack of consistent food on the road was starting to wear on their bodies. Jonathon and Selma were the youngest of them all and even he, at only forty-six years old, was wondering if maybe they should start considering settling down.

They ventured all over Tarlatan, stopping in villages and bringing not only education to all, but resources to the poor. Depending on how severe the situation, Jonathon and his group might stay for up to a year. Other villages might only require a few weeks or months. Sometimes they helped bring children from one village to another, where there would be better education.

But here, in Clearford... Children raced in the streets, ducking under horses and laughing as shopkeepers raised their fist at them. Jonathon smiled- he remembered how it felt to be that young.

"One of yours?" A woman came out of the shop that he leaned against, arms crossed against her chest. He stood a little straighter and admired the woman. Her brown eyes sparkled in the daylight and her lips, despite being pressed tightly together, revealed a small smile.

Jonathon chuckled and shook his head. "No, not one of mine. I'm just passing through. It's nice watching them be so carefree. I remember being their age. My childhood wasn't always easy." He watched them crash down into a laughing heap over by who he assumed were their parents. He chuckled at the sight as the children jumped up and started all over again, playing hide and seek this time. "Jonathon, my lady." The woman next to him shook her head and chuckled a little as well.

"Yvette. My family has owned this shop nigh on three decades now. I've grown up here, played in the streets these kids played in. I remember being able to be so carefree. But our family faced hard times, and we had to resort to some... Unsavory methods to keep the shop afloat. I share the same sentiment." Yvette loosened her arms and walked back inside the shop. Jonathon watched her quickly plait her loose brown hair into a braid, keeping it out of the way as she cleaned the shop.

A child crashed into his legs, knocking him back against the building. "Easy there." Jonathon chided, helping the child up.

"Thank you, sir!" The child pipped, before eagerly running away.

The child's mother, however, had other ideas. "Remus! Apologize this moment. All the children! The market is no place for these games." She yelled out to the kids. Remus stopped in his tracks, turning back to Jonathon with rosy cheeks. The mother yelled towards Jonathon now at her spot a few stalls down. "Apologies, sir. It's difficult when it's still too early to harvest. The kids won't go back to school until after the harvest."

"I apologize, sir. I should have watched where I was going." Remus stood with his head down, hands together behind his back. The children gathered behind Remus, nodding in agreement.

Jonathon waved a hand and knelt down. "'Tis but a scratch. I've dealt with worse on my adventures."

With that, Remus lit up. "You're an adventurer? You've gotta tell us a story!" The kids chorused behind him, pleading for a story. The mother scolded the children, quieting them down.

"Would you like to hear the story of a child who discovered a dragon could have a soul, and adventured all over Tarlatan?" Jonathon smiled a little, nodding to the mother and shrugging his shoulders. The children eagerly plopped onto the ground and Jonathon turned into the shop. "Yvette, I don't supposed you have a stool I could borrow?"

Yvette nodded, and brought Jonathon out a stool. "If this stool doesn't come back, I'll charge double it's worth."

"Of course, my lady." Jonathon smiled and took his seat,

taking out a pouch for snacks and his waterskin. "Now, I suppose I should start at the beginning..."

Jonathon spoke for a quite a while, speaking about how his feet pitter pattered into the cave. The children gasped at the red dragon and widened their eyes at the destruction of Gruffenberg. To them, it was a cautionary tale, he supposed. The children didn't realize he was the boy in the story and... Jonathon thought that was a good thing. Maybe they could believe there was still hope in this world if they had not yet seen men act like that.

Across the road, his group waved to him from the Tavern. Jonathon waved back and signaled that he would be in later. The children gasped in excitement, barely able to sit still.

But sit still they did, even as Jonathon detailed the long nights he spent awake as a child with Thermaxas. He remembered those nights clear as day in the aftermath of Gruffenberg. Thermaxas would light fires in his cave at the same time every night, and the children Thermaxas rescued would pitter patter into the cave as Jonathon did that first fateful night.

Thermaxas would roar, breathe fire, and leap down into the depths of his cave before flying triumphantly up. At the time, it had been a welcome distraction for the children, who were still confused as to what was happening. The older children that Thermaxas had rescued understood but, the younger children... Not all had faced the same situation as Jonathon and, even if they had... Some were shielded by their mothers.

Jonathon even remembered his mother following in, wondering where her child went every night. At first she was scared but by the third night she brought in all the mothers.

Looking back on it now, Jonathon supposed they too found some comfort in the distraction Thermaxas provided.

Jonathon went on, describing his adventures through the coastal city he and his mother had settled in. He spoke of the spreading darkness that had even dimmed the light of Luce

Stellarum. It still plagued him to this day, those Sentinels who might never return. The children kept quiet as the same sense of foreboding fell over all of them. Anyone who lived on the continent of Tarlatan had to be a fool if they did not recognize it. During the middle of his story, Jethro had brought him a tankard of ale which Jonathon was very thankful for.

Jonathon was just at the end of describing when he had finally returned to Thermaxas when he noticed Remus' mother waving over to him. He supposed the rest of the story was boring, anyways. He truly hadn't seen Thermaxas since his twenties, and every time his group passed by his cave, the red dragon wasn't there.

Jonathon brushed off his pants and stood as the children returned to running in the streets. He took a sip from the last of his ale and eyed the tavern- in there was a delicious baked potato soup and brisket. His bones creaked and reminded him that although his life had slowed, he would rather take the slower pace than adventuring all day and night constantly. Nothing sounded better than a steamy bowl of soup in front of a warm fire in a comfy chair.

It seemed that the world had other, more *interesting* plans for his day.

Out of the corner of his eye, Jonathon saw a woman come up. She had auburn hair and the tipped ear of the Fae, which she attempted to hide beneath the hood of her cloak. The cloak was pinned with a clasp made of a sword and twisting vines.

"What about the Sentinels? Did they remain lost?" Jonathon shrugged his shoulders at the woman's question.

"Your guess is as good as mine, Lady. I would have thought they would have returned to their Fae ancestors after Luce Stellarum fell, though. People say they're never coming back." Jonathon stood from his stool, beginning to pack his things. Out of the corner of his eye, he watched a dagger fall out of her sleeve.

Jonathon felt for that piece of gold again. He wondered if now might be a good time to call. He peeked inside the store behind him- Yvette was gone, nowhere to be seen.

"We did not return to the Fae. They refused our call for aid." The woman's voice was chilly, as though she still held an anger about it to this day. Remus' mother was gathering the children and huddled them behind her stall. She stared wearily over at Jonathon and the Fae woman.

Jonathon froze, still gripping the piece of gold. He didn't question himself when he sent that frazzled thought down the soul tie.

Rage and comfort rippled in response.

"We, Lady?" Jonathon continued to pack his things as he watched the woman. One of his friends poked his head out the tavern door and Jonathon signaled for him to stay inside.

She nodded her head. "Yes, we. We did not return to the Fae. They betrayed us by not helping us. A few who longed to see their mothers returned, but most did not. I am a Sentinel of the Fallen Kingdom and you *will* bring me to Thermaxas."

"What business do you have with Thermaxas? On whose orders?" It was no point telling the Sentinel that he did not know who Thermaxas was. She already knew that he was the boy in the story and had likely been tracking him for days. It wasn't a fact that he kept quiet but... Having a soul tie with a dragon attracted attention, and Jonathon tended to keep it close to his chest. Whenever he told stories, he never told the listener his name.

But this Sentinel had found him. He just prayed to whatever gods still listened that Thermaxas would, too.

"My business is my own." She stopped circling him. She spun the dagger in her hand, staring him down.

A roar sounded in the distance. The town fell silent and everyone halted. Jonathon smiled- always a grand entrance.

The Sentinel looked at him in disbelief. "You called him?"

"Thermaxas was always protective. He was probably

already flying over." Jonathon smiled, fingering that gold coin again.

The world shook with another roar. As if confirming that he had felt Jonathon's fear and would answer even if he hadn't called.

The Sentinel pulled the sword from her side out and held it loosely, watching Thermaxas circle above before landing outside the city. Jonathon and the Sentinel both walked towards the dragon, dodging people who ran away. Confused screams filled the city, some wondering why he wasn't attacking and others wondering if he was just waiting for them to panic *more*.

Thermaxas loosed a small breath of fire, rage rippling at the soul tie. "The next time you wish to see me, Sentinel, you will not use Jonathon to do so." Jonathon watched Thermaxas, who offered him a smile before baring his teeth at the Sentinel.

The Sentinel did not sheath her sword but did bow, a little. She walked up, much closer than Jonathon would have thought was wise. "Thermaxas, we have an issue. Evil is threatening Tarlatan. My sisters are rallying forces to try and protect kingdoms, but we alone are not enough. We need allies."

"And why would the Sentinels want to ally with Thermaxas the Bloody?" The dragon snorted. Jonathon watched in awe as he witnessed history take place. The Sentinels... They were returning.

The warriors everyone said were gone were returning and Jonathon couldn't tell if he was glad, or if they had stayed hidden. Perhaps the evil would have stayed at bay.

"Because Thermaxas, this evil is so deep rooted even you will not outlast it alone. And I think your ward was correct-you do have a heart and could not bear seeing Jonathon die. Could you imagine that feeling rippling down the soul tie?"

The Sentinel was still close- so close Jonathon saw Thermaxas' breaths blow her hair back.

Thermaxas snarled. "Do not threaten my ward or you will find yourself without a head, Sentinel or not." Jonathon stepped closer. A Sentinel dying would send a message to the entire world, never mind this continent. If Jonathon had to step in, he would.

'Then stop being so broody and meet us in the Ionian mountains." The Sentinel sheathed her sword and pulled out an invitation. The invitation was sealed with wax and stamped with the crest of Rosenfall. Jonathon raised an eyebrow and rushed towards the Sentinel to grab it for Thermaxas.

Thermaxas cocked his head and furrowed his brows. "Who is us?"

The Sentinel wore a wicked smile. "Open the invitation. I think you'll find that it's an... Interesting, team." The Sentinel turned around, heading towards the docks. But she paused her steps and turned her head back slightly towards Jonathon and Thermaxas. "Thermaxas, this continent needs you. This alliance that is being put together... It might not be enough, no matter how powerful my allies may be. I personally requested you and had that invitation rushed here to the docks of Trifillem. When I realized neither of you were near Trifillem, I hunted for Jonathon and found that he was heading towards Clearford. I knew that if I found him, I would find you. I hope I did waste precious time looking for you." She spoke softly, sighed, and continued walking towards the docks.

Jonathon stood there, frozen with the invitation in his hand. Thermaxas nudged him with his nose, hot air rushing at his back.

"Are you alright?" Thermaxas spoke as softly as Jonathon knew he could. The townsfolk stood in the streets, an opening down the center where the Sentinel was walking. They parted the entire way to the docks, until she got on her boat and they sailed away. Jonathon and Thermaxas stood there for a while. Jonathon didn't know how to respond.

Jonathon was a mortal man. Yes- he had a soul tie to a dragon. But… He was a mortal man living during a time where Sentinels were returning and speaking of ancient evils deeply rooted in the lands. How was he supposed to begin to think about that?

Finally, as the sun set over the sea, Jonathon spoke from his spot where he sat against Thermaxas. "You have to go. Not just for me. For this entire continent." Jonathon did not leave any room for Thermaxas to question him.

"Jonathon, we can talk about this lat-" Thermaxas started to speak, but Jonathon interrupted him.

"No, Thermaxas. We open this invitation and talk now. Twenty five years ago, I told you that people were saying the Sentinels would never return. Now one has, personally requesting that *you* join an alliance." Jonathon stared at the invitation in his hand before popping off the wax seal with his thumb.

He opened the envelope and pulled out the letter.

Thermaxas the Bloody-

You are likely wondering who has sent you and why you have been called for. I apologize that this letter will not be enough to describe it to you. You have been called upon by an alliance between the Queens of Luce Stellarum and Rosenfall. A great threat comes from the West, one that threatens the entire world.

We have called upon the greatest powers of this world. Canberran Pirates have joined our call, mythical guardians, and Gods. When our General of the Sentinels, Daenestra, personally requested you, we were hesitant. It is believed that black dragons are under control of the West. Red dragons might not be so different. But you… You are. We trust Daenestra with our lives. Meet us in the Ionian mountains by Winter Solstice. You'll receive more information there.

Jonathon reached the end and threw the invitation down. Thermaxas burned the invitation and the seal, scorching the ground as well. Both of them would never forget what it said, anyways.

Thermaxas spoke first. "Luce Stellarum was destroyed." Jonathon almost felt Thermaxas' shock. "A Queen of Luce Stellarum has returned, and has allied with the Dark Queen of Rosenfall... When Light and Dark are on the same side, what does that say of the enemy?" Thermaxas let out a deep breath. He was staring out towards Clearford, watching the twinkling lights. By this point, the townsfolk had seemingly accepted Thermaxas' presence.

There was laughter, there was yelling, there was crying. But more importantly, there was life. Jonathon watched Thermaxas, watched him stare out at Clearford and take in all the life. Jonathon had never encountered another dragon in his lifetime, but he knew not all were like Thermaxas. Not all appreciated life as Thermaxas did.

"It says that this enemy will have the greatest forces this world has ever seen against it. There is no enemy who could stand a chance, Thermaxas." Jonathon spoke quietly, letting the wind carry his words away. He sent a calming feeling down the soul tie and watched as Thermaxas flung out his wings.

"No matter what happens, Jonathon... No matter where in the world I am, you will always be protected. If I am to join Sentinels, Dark Queens, Pirates, and Gods... You may be a target. So, if you are attacked, call for me. Scream if you have to." Thermaxas paused. "And pray the enemy does not come after you, for they will learn the fire and fury of a red dragon well if they find you." With that, Thermaxas took off running, beating his wings hard. The wind whipped back at Jonathon and he had to brace himself despite his aching knees. A final beat of his wings followed by a leap had Thermaxas in the air, flying fast towards the North and the Ionian Mountains.

Jonathon closed his eyes, and prayed to every god he knew that Thermaxas would live. He did not want to imagine the pain of a soul tie shredding apart. He could not imagine the pain- the thought alone nearly cleaved his own soul in two.

The sky was dark, moon barely lighting the sky. When had the nights become so dark? Everything seemed so dim, even the lights in the town. Jonathon looked over it all and, after reading the letter, had little hope that the light could ever return.

He wondered if this enemy had wiped out Luce Stellarum and burned Hallenfall to the ground. If that enemy had returned...

He blew out his nose, pinched the bridge of it. No, it was too much to think about in one night. So he walked back into town, ignoring the guards who gripped their swords a little harder and stared him down all the way to the tavern.

Remus' mother and the children were all gone by now, her stall boarded up for the night. Yvette's shop was locked and windows closed up, with a sign that noted the opening time tomorrow.

The tavern was still open with light pouring out the windows. Lanterns were lit on the inside with fires blazing in each of the five fireplaces. Candles were lit in every chandelier.

As he walked inside, he dodged the waitresses serving tankards of ale. They whirled around the crowds as if they had done it for years. They held their trays high above the heads of the customers and never spilled a drop. The kitchen doors swung constantly, with a revolving door of waitresses coming in and out with trays of food. Jonathon marveled at it all as he walked over to the table where his friends sat.

"They're busy tonight. Busier than I can remember..." Jonathon interrupted his laughing friends, slumping into his chair.

One of the leaders in their guild, Selma, raised an eyebrow. "Have fun with the dragon? You brought in quite a crowd. People rushed in from the port after the Sentinel left, eager to place bets." Selma caught a bag of gold thrown at her, smiling as she weighed the bag in her hand. It was stuffed into a pack, where he noticed another bag of gold.

Jonathon furrowed his eyebrows. "Place bets? On what?"

"On whether you were, in fact, the Jonathon who had the soul tie with a dragon and if you would come back alive." Jethro chuckled, taking a swig of his ale. "Selma here bet that you would come back alive, and that you were the one with the soul tie. During your escapade with Thermaxas, by the way, we stabled the horses and brought in our things."

Good- Jonathon hadn't even thought about the horses. He was so caught up with Thermaxas and the Sentinel that keeping track of horses was the last thing on his mind.

Jonathon thought back on the group's time together. He had only ever spoken to Jethro about the soul tie. Jonathon hadn't exactly hidden it from the group, but he had never brought it up to them and they had never asked. If he was being honest, after all this time together, he had expected them to find out on their own somehow. A mischievous smile lit up Selma's face and she glanced down at the gold she had placed into the pack.

Selma had been the first in the group that Jethro had recruited. She was not only a master seamstress and tailor, but a trickster and thief at heart. They seldom needed her thieving skills, but the trickster portion helped them gain popularity with children.

Sometimes the parents in the village were all for Jethro's group to come in and assist. They would establish a school, get it started, and help educate in other areas. The children, meanwhile, were often thrown in at the last minute. The parents sent them to the newly built schoolhouse and Selma was the one they first encountered. If they came to school reluctant and moody, they left cheerful and excited for more. Eventually they eased them into actual learning by the time they left so that the next child might be more prepared.

Selma could warm a heart of ice with a simple smile. Sometimes Jonathon wondered if she was the one with a soul tie to a dragon and not him.

"I had a couple thoughts. At best, you come back alive and I get a bag of gold. At worst, you come back dead and I'm stuck one pouch of gold poorer. It was worth the risk." She shrugged her shoulders, smiling at him. Jethro raised his hand, waving down a waitress. He shouted for a tankard of ale and a bowl of the soup.

Jonathon's mouth watered at the sound of the baked potato soup. He had been waiting all night for it- and that Sentinel had delayed it.

"Well, Selma, I'm glad you've been thinking, because I have been too." Jonathon grabbed the tankard and bowl from the waitress that whisked by him. "We're all tired and achy, correct?" Jonathon looked at his group. Jethro and Selma nodded. The other two members of the group, Jyn and Namior, both shrugged their shoulders.

Jyn and Namior were brothers- or so they said. Both came from a town on the edge of Statium. It was suspected they came from the Canberran Caves, ruled only by Statium in terms of borders on maps. The Canberran Caves were truly ruled by the Canberran Pirates, who ruled the Seven Seas as well.

Despite being vigilantes on the sea and terrors in ports, they stuck true to their word and had even assisted in the evacuation of Luce Stellarum. No one dared question the rule of Canberran Pirates- the last King who had done so had lost not only three of their best generals but a head as well.

Jyn and Namior had that same cocky, self righteous attitude that so many Canberran Pirates possessed. But they were the muscle of their group and master craftsmen. They often lead the building of any structure and when it came to the sea, they were the first to be consulted.

Jonathon snorted at the shrug. "Well, *most of us* are tired and achy. Perhaps... Perhaps it's best we settle down."

Selma, unsurprisingly, was the first one to protest. "What about the villages we haven't been to? Why would we settle down?" Despite Selma loving to work with children- she had never wanted any of her own. To Selma, the children she had helped all became her own at one point or another. She enjoyed the freedom of being childless. And now to abandon children she could be helping...

"Jonathon may have a point. We're not getting any younger and we won't be of use to anyone if we die of exhaustion on the road." Jethro spoke, surprising Jonathon. He had suspected that Jethro would have been the next after Selma to pitch a fit. But he had caught Jethro's wince earlier. It was part of the reason Jonathon had brought this up in the first place.

Jyn and Namior shared a look before Jyn spoke. "We've been on the road together for... nearly thirty years. You want to split now? We've all abandoned our families for this. Some of us never got to form other families..." Jyn and Namior had been recruited shortly after Selma. They had been the same age as Jonathon when they were recruited and had wanted adventure.

"Splitting up isn't up for discussion. We're sticking together- end of story. But how will we make money? We've gotten some funds saved, but helping poor villages isn't exactly lucrative." Namior placed his hand on Jyn's shoulder and gripped it tightly.

The tavern around them grew louder, packed in tighter. More and more people were walking in. From what could be heard, these men and women were coming from ships that had just docked for the night. When they heard of the man who attracted not only a Sentinel, but a dragon, and bets were being placed, they rushed from the port to the tavern.

Jonathon dug into his soup, thoroughly enjoying it. There

were crumbled bits of bacon, melted strings of cheese, and green onions all mixed in. It warmed his soul. He sent that warmth down the soul tie, in an attempt to comfort Thermaxas. He could feel the frazzled, shocked energy still rolling off the soul tie.

Jonathon couldn't blame Thermaxas.

"Perhaps if you don't need me to steal, we can use Jonathon here as a prized horse for people to place bets on." Selma grumbled, crossing her arms.

Jonathon rolled his eyes. "Namior is right- splitting up isn't up for discussion. We'd come up with a place to settle down *together.* And Selma... We'll never be able to help everyone. But perhaps if we settle down, we can help in other ways. Jyn, Namior, maybe you can take on apprentices? Selma... Perhaps you can rejoin the Thieve's Den? You've been telling stories of the infamous Thieve's Den for years. Now would be the time to join. You can still be a part of our guild, and help the children that need to earn a little extra money, or get a good start to life. This might be our time." Jonathon paused. "Just... Promise me you'll think about it. That's all I ask."

The grumbles he heard sounded like a vague yes, and he'd take that as a victory for now. Jethro was the only one who nodded and genuinely understood. Jethro was twenty years Jonathon's elder- but it had never stopped him from leading adventures and advocating for journeys even when they would be difficult.

Now that Jethro was getting older... Jonathon supposed relaxing must have sounded like a better idea than it had in the past.

The group finished their ales and soups, some getting drunker than others. Jyn and Namior clambered back up to their rooms, shouldering each other while Selma walked wearily behind them. After making sure the twins were definitely *not* going to fall down the stairs on top of him, Jethro made his way up to his room.

And finally went Jonathon, after grabbing a half a loaf of bread and bringing it up with him to his room. Jyn and Namior had brought in his things at some point throughout the night. When exactly that had been, he wasn't sure. But Jonathon looked around the room at the candle that was almost burned out and the dresser that had seen better days. The food was good here and the rooms were decent...

If they settled down, they wouldn't have to settle for just decent rooms. They could come here simply for the food and go home again.

Jonathon went over to the window and stared for a moment. People were heading back to the docks, stumbling through the streets, and the night market was opening.

The night market was unique to Clearford- every night at the stroke of midnight, the stalls of the market during the day turned into a market at night. Unique items that couldn't be sold during the day- clandestine, rare, stolen, and seductive- appeared here in the stalls. Lanterns were strung across the streets from shop to shop and fireflies came in from the forest. They twinkled in the streets, lighting the alleyways that were untouched by the lanterns.

This- this was what drew him to this place all those years ago, when he had to leave Trifilem and start a life of his own. He spent one night in Clearford and knew that he wanted to be there. It was magical to watch, no matter how old you were.

The drunkards who stumbled back to the docks ignored the stalls- but fresh ships came into the port.

Pirates, he murmured to himself. Canberran Pirates- he recognized them by their thick, cream shirts that were more tan than cream on a good day and the blue pants that were loose on the thighs but wrapped tightly around the calves with string. On land they wore laced up, leather, calf high boots that almost completely hid the tightly wrapped pants.

The Canberran now frequented the blacksmith shop

Jonathon had apprenticed at when they came to the ports of Clearford. They didn't pillage or plunder Clearford, no- they spent their gold here. They were the largest buyers at the Night Market and stopped at the beginning of each month to see the new products.

Different Pirate Lords came around with parts of the fleet at different times at the beginning of the month. Each night for the first week was dominated by the Canberran Pirates. Jonathon idly wondered if he should tell Jyn and Namior that the pirates were here- perhaps they might recognize someone.

Perhaps they might recognize family. Jyn was right- most of them had given up their family to join this rag tag guild of adventurers. Jethro hadn't promised them gold... Only a chance to make the world a better place, and that was enough for any of them.

Jonathon thought back to his mother, who was still living in Trifillem. He still wrote to her faithfully and told her where to send her letters to, so that he could receive them. He'd always tell her the town that they were journeying to, so he'd have her letters when he got there.

Much like Jyn and Namior had abandoned their family, he abandoned his mother. She understood, and ensured him she didn't feel that he abandoned her. The pain of leaving her never left his soul though, and a permanent ache had settled that even Thermaxas couldn't soothe.

His adventures weren't like living in Clearford. Clearford was a day's journey from Trifillem. If he started in the early morning, he could be in Trifillem by dinner time. But when he adventured across the continent, he couldn't just stop off in Clearford.

Enough. Enough for tonight. You can see her soon. Jonathon shook his head, pulling himself away from the window. Yes, he would see her soon. Tomorrow was a new day.

CHAPTER 2

A NEW LIFE

J onathon awoke with a twinge of a headache and his muscles sorer than they had been yesterday, if that was possible. He hadn't even gotten that drunk, but he supposed his age was starting to creep up on him.

He wasn't a warrior after all- only a teacher who rode a horse.

He groaned, rubbing his eyes and pushing himself off the bed. His feet hit the floor harder than he would have liked, and his back complained as he bent forward.

One thing I won't miss about adventuring is the shitty beds at half rate taverns. Jonathon thought to himself, grumbling as he tugged on his shoes.

There was a knock at the door. "Are you up, old man? We're going to explore the market and see what's fresh at the docks!" Selma yelled through the door, sounding as though she was bouncing on her feet. Jonathon knew she was itching to practice her pickpocketing skills. Jethro liked to keep a respectable guild, but in large cities like this, it was ripe with opportunity.

"I'll be outside in a minute, Selma." Jonathon chuckled, shaking his head. He tugged on a new shirt and belted his pants before slipping his feet into his boots and lacing them up. He grabbed a satchel and slipped it over his head before running out the door, barely giving himself time to actually open it.

He rushed through the halls of the inn and the dining room of the tavern before getting outside. Selma was tapping her foot with her arms crossed, while Jyn and Namior eyed an armory across the street. Jethro simply smoked his pipe, sitting on a bench.

"Here I was, thinking I was the old man. Meanwhile I've had time to eat breakfast *and* smoke a pipe while waiting for you all." Jethro raised an eyebrow, putting out his pipe and storing it in his pocket. Jonathon snorted, walking out into the street.

"You'll also go to bed the earliest tonight, Jethro. Don't fool yourself." Jonathon poked, earning a grin from Selma. Jethro stood, seeming to ignore Jonathon and pulling a piece of paper out of his pocket.

"Well, now that we're all up and ready to go, I think we should split up for the day. Jyn and Namior, you'll inspect our tools and weapons. If they're not in good shape, either get them repaired or buy new ones. See if the blacksmith will give us a deal if we give him our old weapons and tools. Selma, your job is to look over our stores. See where we're lacking and buy enough to last us for two weeks. We'll add to them when we know we're leaving. If you see anything worth bartering for, be a fox. Jonathon and I will scope out Clearford for any real estate worth looking at." Jethro ran through his list.

"Real estate?" Jyn paused, the gears in his head turning. "We didn't agree to stay here."

"I know, Jyn. But if we are going to consider it, we want to know what we're getting into. It's just scoping the town and surrounding village out." Jethro walked over towards Jonathon, putting a hand on Jonathon's shoulder. He looked

Jyn dead in the eyes with a huge grin on his face. "Besides, the woman you met last night at the market might want you to stay."

Jyn's mouth opened wide before he scoffed. "It was two women! Don't discount me." Namior patted Jyn on the back, nodding in approval.

Selma rolled her eyes. "While you boys keep count, I'm going to go and scope out how deep the pockets of this town really run." She disappeared into the steadily growing crowd, heading somewhere down an alley. Jyn and Namior went off to the barns, where their tools and weapons were stored in a locked chest.

Which left Jonathon and Jethro standing together.

"Let's walk, Jonathon." Jethro took off, forcing Jonathon to catch up to him.

It was a marvel, Clearford. There was one main entrance, to make it easier to defend. From the entrance, was a street that led straight down to the docks, twisting ever so slightly to the right. The further they ventured down that Main Street, the taller the buildings grew, nearly closing in on one another at the very top.

Down some alleyways, the buildings completely joined together at the top forming tunnels and passageways while others were joined by rope bridges. Clearford was a sprawling maze once you got into alleyways. Shops and homes were intermingled, no one clear district for anything except on the Main Street.

Street vendors littered the corners, selling everything from meat on a stick to cheap jewelry and trinkets. Something to pawn off on people coming in from the docks or travelers like Jethro and Jonathon. Everything else beyond the meat on a stick and trinkets were items bartered for with traders coming off the docks and adventurers looking to sell their wares.

The ultimate motto in Clearford was that if you didn't want to see something sketchy at a stall, you shouldn't have been walking down a dark alleyway in the first place. If it was being sold on the Main Street, it was deemed worthy by the Town Manager, who took daily strolls through the day market.

"What happened with Thermaxas?" Jethro pulled Jonathon out of his observations as they peered at stalls and up at apartments. Some had windows thrown open with clothes hanging on a string that went from one side of the street to the other.

So *that* was the string that the lanterns were hung up on.

Jonathon blew out a deep breath. "A Sentinel approached Thermaxas. She warned him of a great evil that threatened the world." Jonathon pinched the bridge of his nose, shaking his head. "I still feel his stress and frustration. I know he doesn't mean to throw it all down the soul tie- but it ends up there, and it's all I can feel sometimes."

Jethro stopped, went completely still, before walking forward again. "Sentinels? Luce Stellarum was lost- their Sentinels thought dead, or gone to never return. They have no Queen to call them back." Jethro murmured quietly, not that anyone was paying attention to them. The streets may have been getting thicker by the minute, but everyone else was so wrapped up in their own conversation or travels that they didn't pay attention to Jethro and Jonathon.

"The Queen of Luce Stellarum has returned- and she has allied with the Dark Queen of Rosenfall." Jonathon spoke even lower. So low, he doubted Jethro could even hear him. But the old man sputtered in shock, and Jonathon knew that Jethro had heard.

"I see why you mentioned settling down here now. It wasn't just the sore muscles, then?" Jethro questioned. Jonathon nodded, keeping quiet. He had told the truth- he felt the stress rolling off Thermaxas. He felt the stress of keeping a lid on the soul tie, not trying to let all of his stress rumble through. But Jonathon felt it all, and knew Thermaxas felt Jonathon's own worry.

Jonathon stopped at an apartment on the corner of an alley and the Main Street. It was marked for rent, with the door boarded up and flyers in the mail slot in the door.

"If the world ends... I would like to enjoy my last few years in peace. I would like to spend it close to my mother, in a town where there is something for all of us." Jonathon sat on a bench, with Jethro sitting next to him. Jonathon unrolled the flyer, reading the apartment description. The first floor was marked as business, able to be rented out to a business owner or used by the owner. The second and third floors were residential, able to be lived in by the owner or rented out. There was one kitchen, with three bedrooms and, by some marvel, a privy with working piping.

It was a marvel that Clearford wasn't on more maps. But they weren't an ambitious people. No, they were content to keep their town small and protect it from outsiders. If Clearford was left alone, they would leave everyone else alone.

Jethro took the flyer from Jonathon and mulled it over. "I'll get a word into the current owner, see what the price is. I've saved up quite a bit of gold, in case we did want to settle down. Do you-" Jethro was interrupted by kids running up to Jonathon, screaming in delight. Remus led the group, jumping up and down.

"You're still here! We saw the dragon. It was the most exciting thing we've ever seen! You have to tell us more about your journeys." Remus sat down and the children behind him joined. Jonathon laughed with Jethro, both shaking their heads.

"I'm afraid I've told you all of my adventures with Thermaxas. The rest is the boring adventures of a mortal man, surely you wouldn't be interested in those..." Jonathon shrugged his shoulders and moved to stand, but Remus blocked him from going anywhere.

"No, we want to hear the stories! We want to hear how

you got here!" Remus pleaded with Jonathon, looking him in the eyes and pouting.

Jethro shouldered Jonathon. "We have time. I don't mind sitting here with you."

Jonathon looked at the children once more before smiling. "Well, I suppose I should start when I too was a child, after Thermaxas had rescued the women and children of Gruffenberg…

⚜

'THE FOREST AROUND THE CAVE OF THERMAXAS WAS THE safest place Jonathon had ever felt. He was comforted by the loud snores of Thermaxas during the day, and his form patrolling the skies above at night. He heard the loud flaps of his wings, cracking like thunder. Jonathon supposed Thermaxas wasn't a stealthy hunter, but the dragon didn't need stealth when he had fire.

It had been two months since Thermaxas had rescued the women and children. The women spent the first couple weeks adjusting to their new lives, trying to figure out what living- not just surviving- felt like.

The nights that Thermaxas did not spend patrolling, he spent entertaining the children while the women had their meetings. Jonathon pitter pattered into the cave, much like he had over two months ago now. Children followed behind him, their footsteps echoing off the walls of the cave. Thermaxas snored, curled up into a ball and his tail draped across his nose.

Jonathon tiptoed up to him, a smile appearing on the boy's face. Thermaxas snored loudly, causing Jonathon to pause. But Jonathon continued after a moment, deeming Thermaxas still asleep. And when he got close enough…

"Boo!" Jonathon whisper yelled at Thermaxas, causing the

dragon to lurch up in surprise. The dragon rolled over onto his back, letting his wings out a bit.

"I surrender! You've got me!" Thermaxas roared, laughing with puffs of smoke coming from his nostrils. Thermaxas' eyes met Jonathon's, and they shared a smile, both eyes filled with genuine happiness. The children behind them were laughing, huddled together.

It had been the same routine for the past two months. Thermaxas would pretend to sleep, Jonathon would practice his sneaking and try to startle Thermaxas. It was a part of Jonathon's training, Thermaxas told him. If Jonathon could get past a sleeping dragon, he could get past any danger. Thermaxas had offered the same to the other children, but no one had taken him up on it as far as Jonathon knew.

Jonathon's mother cleared her throat behind all the children. Thermaxas rolled back onto his stomach and bowed his head towards her. "My lady. Your son has gotten quite good at sneaking as of late. I apologize if we disturbed your meeting." Thermaxas kept his head bowed for another moment before lifting it up. The other women filled into the cave behind Jonathon's mother.

"It's no worries, Thermaxas. We decided that we didn't need a meeting tonight, and wanted to join you in here with the children. Would that be alright?" Jonathon's mother asked, walking up to be next to her son. Jonathon smiled, bouncing on his feet. He knew at some point they would have to leave… But if they had to stay, that wouldn't be so bad either.

"It's no worries at all, Isabel. Please, follow me. We can get started a little early tonight, if you'd like." Thermaxas turned, and Jonathon nearly questioned why there was a tear falling down his face. But Jonathon didn't question it, because when his mother had cried, he had learned that questioning had gone nowhere.

Questioning almost always ended up with Jonathon crying too. Perhaps… Perhaps if Jonathon didn't question it, he wouldn't end up crying this time. Perhaps the happiness would stay forever.

And happy Jonathon was. Thermaxas led the women and children deeper into his cave, past the piles of gold and the stores of food. He led them to the caverns, where it opened up into huge cave systems and vast caverns. It was large enough for Thermaxas to spread his wings wide and spin in circles. Thermaxas dove deep into the cavern, turning at the last minute and flapping his wings hard. The sound echoed through the caves like an explosion, causing the children to *oooh* and *aaah*.

Thermaxas roared fire, lighting up the dark cavern. He angled it towards torches along the wall, lighting them as he flew past. The light glinted off his red scales, bathing them in gold. His golden eyes burned brightly, turning almost blue as the fire heated more and more in his soul.

And that fire, that burned so brightly in his soul, exploded out of his mouth and lit the caverns of four other caves at the bottom. The children peered down, admiring the lake at the bottom that glistened. Creatures lounged on the edge of the lake, staring up at Thermaxas as he performed his act. The children had never questioned the creatures, confident that Thermaxas would keep them safe.

Jonathon liked to think that the creatures enjoyed the show as much as him and the rest of the children did.

This wasn't the first time their mothers and the other women had joined the children in watching Thermaxas. But as Thermaxas swooped up and landed gently next to the women, Jonathon noticed the tears in Thermaxas' eyes threaten to burst. Somewhere within Jonathon's soul, he felt such an intense sadness that he too felt like he might cry.

Thermaxas' eyes were still blue, but cooling back to gold as they met Jonathon's. A wall flew up in his soul, cutting off any sadness. Instead, happiness trickled in, urging the sadness to go away.

Jonathon's mother stood next to Thermaxas, with the other women behind her.

"We have come to a decision." Jonathon froze at his mother's words. No- they couldn't have, it was to soon. "A little under half of our group will be heading towards the small fishing village. They have agreed to take in a certain number of women and children. We've discussed who will stay together. That group will be lead under Gemella, who will stay with you until you reach the village. From there, she will continue onto Velletia. The rest of the group will be lead under me. We will go to Trifillem, the coastal city Theramaxas recommended. Trifillem and its neighboring town, Clearford, are ripe with trade. The group under me will be able to decide which town they would like to settle in." Jonathon's mother looked around at all the children, her eyes finally landing on Jonathon.

Jonathon almost wished she hadn't looked at him. Her look of pity as she looked at him, knowing how happy he had been these past couple of months, nearly crippled him. Jonathon burst out of the cavern, running through the tunnels and towards the forest.

Between him running and the tears falling down his face, the walls of the cave blurred around him. One moment he was in the cave and the next he ran out into the forest, the moon shining brightly.

He heard someone following him. Likely his mother- although he didn't care. He knew that they had to leave at some point... But did it have to be so soon?

"Leave me alone." Jonathon grumbled, sliding down the back of a tree and hitting the ground. He hugged his knees and kept his head hidden, the tears continuing to fall.

His mother sat in front of him, placing her hand on his foot. "Do you want to talk about what's happening?" Jonathon's mother spoke softly, gently.

"I don't want to talk." Jonathon scrunched up more, trying to make himself smaller.

"Jonathon, look at me." His mother wouldn't leave. He didn't think he wanted her too, but he was supposed to be her brave boy. Brave boys didn't cry. His mother moved her hand from his foot to underneath his chin, making Jonathon look up at her.

Jonathon tried not to cry more and tried to shake her hand off. But his mother gripped his chin, forcing him to look at her.

"Did you not want me to see you cry?" Jonathon's mother, despite her grip on his chin, spoke in a whisper and was so gentle, he might have forgotten her holding him. He nodded, hugging his knees tighter. "Jonathon... Do not ever fear someone seeing you cry."

His mother let go of his chin and sat criss crossed in front of him. "Do you know how proud I am of you? You ran off for two weeks. A week you were by yourself. You journeyed for a week to find Thermaxas, the vicious red dragon I told you about. And somehow, you found a soul in that dragon. Crying doesn't make you any less brave or any less worthy of pride. Crying means you feel something- *anything*- and if someone says that showing you feel something is wrong... Well, the gods should take pity on them. Girl or boy, crying doesn't make you less than anyone else." Jonathon's mother wiped the tear from his face and kissed his forehead.

"I don't want to leave Thermaxas, Momma." Jonathon whispered, the words feeling like they ripped his soul to pieces. He didn't *want to leave.*

"I know sweetheart. But you need to go to school, and I need to find a job. We won't be far from Thermaxas. And a part of you will always live with the other. Your souls are *tied* together." Jonathon's mother ruffled his hair and stood up, holding her hand out. She helped Jonathon up off the ground and they walked back into the cave.

"Did Thermaxas know?" Jonathon questioned, looking up at his mother. She nodded and Jonathon leaned against her as they walked. The children walked out past them, with the mothers behind them. Thermaxas was sitting in the cavern, with fresh tears rolling down his cheeks. Jonathon pitter pattered up to him, and poked his snout. "Momma says we don't have to hide our tears."

His mother and Theramaxas chuckled. "Isabel is a wise woman. You have a wonderful mother, Jonathon. I wasn't hiding my tears before- I just didn't want to scare you. I will miss you more than you know." Thermaxas nuzzled Jonathon with his snout, and motioned for Jonathon and his mother to sit next to him. They could see down into the cave below, with torches still lit on the wall down to the bottom of the cavern. The water was lit, with quiet splashing from the creatures.

"What are they?" Jonathon asked, peering down into the cavern below. He could barely make out their features, only seeing that they were gray and looked like a man and woman.

"Those are the mer. In truth, they are more fish than human. They are grayish creatures with scaly skin. Some say they used to be water nymphs and the god Aquetious cast them into this cave when they betrayed him. Their upper bodies resemble man, but their hair has been turned to long scales and their eyes are slitted. If you ever get close enough, you'll notice that they not only have webbed fingers, but instead of feet and legs have tails." Thermaxas explained them to Jonathon, all three of them watching the creatures below.

"Is it just you and them that live in this cave? Did they ever have any friends?" Jonathon's mother asked, crossing her legs and leaning back a little.

Thermaxas hummed, thinking for a moment. "There used to be some creatures here long ago. The last of them migrated to the west hundreds of years ago, and haven't been seen since. My mother told me stories of them. They were called phantoms. My mother explained that the phantoms are nearly white, some ivory and some cream colored. All phantoms were blind, or so it was rumored. They had a greater since of smell than even I, and a greater prey drive too. Some were horned, but their feathers and wings stole the show. My mother said some used to sparkle like starlight, they were so bright." Themaxas paused. "I am a dragon and I can fly. But the phantoms... Their wings were thirty feet from tip to tip and had their own soul. They bristled with movement even when tucked in. Dragons envied the phantoms for having such a relationship with their wings. Now they are bedtime stories, told to dragons like me who will never see a phantom."

Jonathon tried to imagine the phantoms and their beautiful wings. Thermaxas was scaled and thick, his dragon hide prized on the black market. But these phantoms sounded ethereal for being skilled hunters.

Jonathon tugged on his mother's dress. "Momma, can I stay with Thermaxas for the night?" He peered into her eyes, hoping she would say yes. To his excitement, she did say yes, and he would have jumped for joy if the edge of the cave was not so near.

"I will watch over him, Isabel. If any of you need anything, just shout. I will be there in a moments notice." Thermaxas bowed to Jonathon's mother, showing her the utmost respect he could. Jonathon's mother ruffled his hair and kissed his forehead.

Jonathon watched as she walked out of the cave to the rest of the mothers and the children. Thermaxas and Jonathon went to the front hall, where there was a small hole on the wall that served as a fireplace. He pushed some wood that had been gathered by the mothers into the fireplace and breathed sparks onto it. It lit quickly, crackling to life.

The shadows danced on the cave walls, flipping and spinning like wild tornados. Jonathon laid on the ground, curling next to Thermaxas. The dragon curled around him and

Jonathon noticed the fire was hardly needed, with the heat of Thermaxas.

"Thermaxas?" Jonathon whispered. Thermaxas peered an eye open, looking down at the boy. "I am scared to leave you."

The dragon nuzzled Jonathon. "You have no need to be scared. I will never be more than a shout's length away. Tug on your end of the soul tie... And I will come. If anyone threatens you and I am not there yet, tell them you have a soul bond with Thermaxas the Bloody." Thermaxas sighed, closing his eye again. "I have never had children, Jonathon. I have never known what it feels like to love something so deeply that you would do anything for it... Until you came along. So do not fear, Jonathon."

Thermaxas soon settled into snores, leaving Jonathon awake, staring at the shadows dancing on the ceiling.

Jonathon wasn't sure what to think about this new life. He had never known love aside from his mother. His father...

He did not want to think of his father. A beast so retched that a dragon seemed like a hero rather than a deadly monster.

And, somehow, Jonathon drifted to sleep, unknowing of the beast whose other eye remained open and soul remained afire.

The next day, Jonathon woke just after dawn. The rest of their group was already up and going, children wiping at bleary eyes. Mothers were packing and the older children were helping take down tents while cooking breakfast. Jonathon's mother motioned him over, pulling closed their packs.

"Jonathon, our group is about to move out for Trifillem. Are you ready?" His mother was organizing the children and mothers of their half going to Trifillem. They must have packed last night- for all of their belongings were together.

He looked back into the cave, seeing Thermaxas come walking out. Jonathon looked back towards his mother before running towards Thermaxas and throwing himself at his snout. He embraced the dragon, committing the feel of his scales to memory.

"I love you too, Thermaxas." Jonathon pulled back, looking up at Thermaxas. The dragon nuzzled him, large tears falling down his face.

"You will always have your mother, Jonathon. And should you want a father, I will always be here." Thermaxas turned around, walking back into the cave until Jonathon could no longer see him.

Jonathon turned around, going to walk back towards his mother. As he lifted his foot, a gold coin went flying. He ran up to it, grabbing it off the ground and inspecting it. Half the coin looked to be in good condition, but the other half was squished, imprinted by one of Thermaxas' scales.

"Jonathon!" His mother called out, calling him towards her. Jonathon looked up, blinking in surprise. He looked back down at the coin and towards his mother again.

Jonathon pocketed the coin, running towards his mother. He grasped her hand and pulled on the two packs she handed to him. It weighed him down, but he had to be honest...

The thrill of exploration greatly outweighed anything that weighed upon him- physical or emotional.

"Momma, when we get to Trifillem, where will we stay?" Jonathon questioned. He watched the forest pass by as their group walked. The sun was slowly rising, turning the morning sky all different hues of purple and pink and red.

The birds slowly began to chirp, waking with the rest of the world. Squirrels began bouncing from tree to tree while rabbits dashed across the path in front of them.

His mother ruffled his hair. "We have all been welcomed to a woman's shelter. Thermaxas provided a large sum of gold for a donation. The people who run the shelter have said that there is plenty of opportunity in Trifillem." Jonathon nodded and with that- rushed back to the children, joking and playing as they walked. The mothers shared songs and stories that they learned as children.

The day passed into night and continued on, for seven days straight. For the younger children, this was an exciting adventure after leaving the safety of Thermaxas. For the older children, the further they moved from Gruffenberg, the lighter they became.

The mothers, meanwhile, had grown accustomed to living on the road. They had learned how to make traps and how to gather food from the woods. Thermaxas had certainly ensured that they had enough supplies to last them the journey- but the women enjoyed their work, finding life in the land.

One night, the children had decided they would camp together, separate from the mothers. They built their own campfire, hungrily eating before it. The mothers chatted at their own fire, washing dishes and mending clothing.

"When do you think we'll return home?" One child questioned. He was the same age as Jonathon, only five years old.

An older child, perhaps eight, was the one to answer grumpily. "Never. That old dragon stole us away. Mother says it was for the best, but we had a roof over our heads at home. Now we sleep on the tough ground outside."

Jonathon bristled. That was *his* old dragon that the older boy was talking about. "You would have rather let your papa treat you like an animal?" Jonathon questioned.

The older boy snorted. "It was his duty. He had to make sure the household was being run smoothly." The other children around him glanced at each other, before raising their spoons and throwing a glob of stew at him.

Another younger child walked up to the older boy, with his bowl shaking in his hands.

The bowl was turned upside down on the boy's head, the entirety of his stew falling down the older boy's shirt.

The mothers ran over, wondering what was going on as

the older boy yelled, but that younger boy just stood there, with tears falling down his face.

"I am not an animal. My Papa was a monster- just like yours. I feel sorry for you if you can't see that." The younger child was pulled away by his mother, and the older boy's mother took him to get cleaned up.

Jonathon smiled to himself, eating the rest of his stew quietly. The rest of the night was much quieter, but it was the most peaceful the children had felt in… Years.

And finally, one day, they came upon Trifillem. It was so much larger than Gruffenberg and for many, the new possibilities excited them. The city was bustling, with no walls to close it in. As their group explored the city, they peaked into butchers and taverns. Shops lined the streets, with apartments surrounding them. The streets may have been dirty and the buildings slightly neglected, but it was a chance at a new start and the group would take it.

Isabel led Jonathon and the rest of the group to the shelter, where three women rushed out. The building was much taller than all the rest and certainly much wider, taking up nearly half the block on the alleyway. The walls were a dark brick, dotted with stained glass windows and dark painted shutters. Lanterns were hung on either side of the double doors.

The print shop across the street was busy- workers fluttered around inside, paper flying about. Paper boys ran in and out, pockets jingling with change. Some of the boys were barely older than Jonathon.

"We welcome you to the Trifillem Women and Children's Shelter for Lost Souls. My name is Clarissa Downings, and I own the shelter. To my right is Helena Goodspeak, who manages the kitchens and to my left is Prudence Shireborn, who manages the events and staffing outreach. Together, the three of us manage the living quarters and new intakes. We hope your journey here was not too hard?" Clarissa bowed

her head a little, and waved her hand towards the door,
motioning for the group to enter.

Those packs on Jonathon's shoulders and the weight on
the soul tie felt like nothing as he walked into the room. The
front hall was wide and open, with a large staircase leading to
the second floor where on either side of that main staircase
were two leading to a third floor. The sun streamed in through
the stained glass and painted the nearly perfect white walls a
rainbow of colors.

His mother spoke, grabbing Clarissa's hands. "Thank you.
You have no idea how much this second chance means to us."
Clarissa grabbed his mother's hands and clutched them close
to her chest.

"Do not thank us. You were the ones brave enough to
travel here." Clarissa smiled, letting go of his mother's hands
and walking to the front of the staircase. "Here you shall find
your safety and salvation. Your rooms are on the third floor
and the east wing of the second floor. On the west wing on the
second floor are your classrooms, library, and common areas
for studying. On the first floor you have laundry rooms,
kitchens, common areas, and a gymnasium. Behind this staircase is a door out to our gardens, in the atrium. They are free
to browse and pick at, as long as you take care of the gardens.
Please explore the shelter. You will find your room assignments
in the mailboxes in the room to our right." Clarissa bowed
once more before walking away with Helena and Prudence
following her.

Jonathon turned to his mother, who was beaming. "Is this
our home now, Momma? Do we have to leave- will Papa come
back for us?" He had felt it lingering in the back of his head.
Things surely couldn't be this good.

His mother knelt down and bear hugged him. "This is our
home now, Jonathon. We don't have to worry about Papa- we
have a whole new life ahead of us."

JONATHON CLEANED HIS THROAT, TAKING A LONG SWIG FROM his water pouch. The children clapped around him, and Jethro clapped a hand on his shoulder.

"Well children, I suppose we should be on our way. We wouldn't want to keep you from your mothers and fathers, now would we, Jethro?" Jonathon turned to the old man, who was looking at him with pride in his eyes.

Thermaxas would always be more than a father to Jonathon. Thermaxas was a part of Jonathon's soul and Jonathon a part of his. Jethro… Jethro was a constant father figure, someone who had taught Jonathon what it meant to be a good man.

"Can we hear the rest of the story?" Remus begged, not daring to get up. Jonathon laughed- he remembered times at the shelter when his tutors would have to be dragged from the room by staff because the children would not let the tutors leave.

"I'm afraid we do have to go. But perhaps, if you are back tomorrow at the same time, I can continue the story?" Jonathon stood up, helping Jethro off the bench. The children dispersed, running through the streets of Clearford. Jonathon thought back to Trifillem, and his first time there. Clearford was ten times more crowded than Trifillem.

In Trifillem, it was far more open. As a boy, he could see the sea from nearly every point in the city and the saltwater was a part of his body while living there. Here, the city was so congested that Jonathon went to bed having scrubbed off more mud than saltwater.

Jethro and Jonathon continued walking through the city, determined to investigate further and find more properties to share with the group.

"You know, my boy, perhaps if we rented that apartment, we could run a bookstore out of the first floor. There is plenty of opportunity for fresh books from the surrounding cities and there are plenty of children to listen to your own stories." Jethro paused. "I am proud of you Jonathon, for everything you have overcome. I would not be the man I am today without you."

"Thank you, Jethro. I do not want to imagine what my life may have been like without you. I think it was fate, you ordering from that blacksmith shop I apprenticed at." Jonathon smiled.

Jonathon felt down the soul tie, feeling for Thermaxas. He hit a wall of adamant black, as if Thermaxas had thrown walls up to prevent Jonathon from getting in.

He felt for a crack, knowing Thermaxas would have left one. Because no matter how far Thermaxas was, no matter what battle he was in… Thermaxas would have rose from the dead if Jonathon needed him.

Jonathon found a single, solitary crack. He sent a calming feeling through that crack, feeling the wall come down just a little bit.

This was a new life for all of them. No evil would take that opportunity.

CHAPTER 3

DESTINY IS NOT FOR
THE WEAK

Destiny was not for the weak- that much Jonathon had learned in his lifetime.

Time and time again, Jonathon had proved himself to everyone who challenged him. He tore down their walls, revealing their monstrosities to the world. If someone tried to beat him back, he slammed against them like a tidal wave.

Jonathon had learned a long time ago that to be weak was to be naive. The gods watched and plucked those who would not accept their destiny off the continent, one by one. They did not discriminate by age, wealth, or power.

To survive on Tarlatan was to become the best version of yourself, forged in the fires of magic and monsters.

Some did not face their destiny until much later in life, when they had already lived it. Others faced it much earlier on, like Jonathon.

Others like Selma, Jyn, and Namior had yet to face their destiny and Jonathon knew... Jonathon knew in the coming months that might change.

He had faced his own destiny and survived. Watching

others blissfully live without the stress of facing their own destiny was the most anxious part of his life.

Perhaps that was why he was so intent on settling. Maybe they could enjoy a brief respite from destiny if they settled. Perhaps this would be their destiny.

Jonathon and his group were huddled around a table, scarfing down eggs, toast, and sausage. It was no baked potato soup, but it would have to do.

"I'd like to show you all this apartment and tell me what you think. It's for sale, with the lower floor set up for a business and the upper floors designated for residential purposes. We would not all stay in the same place forever, but it would always be open to you all." Jethro pulled out the flyer for the apartment he and Jonathon had stopped at yesterday.

They had continued to venture around the city yesterday, but nothing had seemed quite as appealing as that first apartment. Jethro had contacted the owner to see if they might be able to view it and, by some stroke of luck, it was still available. The owner lived within the city and would be able to show them today.

Jonathon knew it would be perfect timing- he could tell the children stories and after, view the apartment with Jethro. They would be purchasing it jointly.

Even if the group did not decide to stay in Clearford forever, it would be a good place to be able to stay in while visiting... And perhaps, in the future, settle down in.

"When are you going to see it?" Selma grumbled. She was still iffy about it. Jyn and Namior were coming around... But Selma enjoyed life on the road.

"Four o'clock. Gives us enough time to get back and eat dinner before the tavern's rush." Jethro explained. Jonathon knew just as well as Jethro that if food was at risk, the group would never go. "We'll be seeing it anyway. We're heading down after breakfast- Jonathon here's been telling stories to the neighborhood children." Jethro continued to shovel the eggs and sausage into his mouth.

"We're heading down to the ship yard today. They've been doing some interesting repairs on vessels and offered to show us around the yard. I suppose they could also use some help with heavy lifting- but we'll be there at four o'clock." Jyn explained for him and Namior. Jonathon felt relief sear through him.

It was good. They were making connections and getting to know people in Clearford. All was hopefully not lost after all.

"I met a woman yesterday- Yvette. She's a trap and small arms dealer in town. Word around town also says she runs the Thieve's Den at night. I didn't venture out last night, but I may tonight." Selma ate the last of her toast and pushed the plate away.

Yvette? The stool- The thought clanged in Jonathon's mind, his eyes widening at the realization. He had completely forgotten about the stool he had borrowed from Yvette that first day they had gotten into Clearford. Had he given her stool back? If she ran a Thieve's Guild... He had a feeling she'd do more than charge him it's worth.

"You didn't seem to notice her talking about a missing stool?" Jonathon gulped, hiding it by drinking the coffee. Selma shook her head, getting up out of the seat.

"No, no mention of a missing stool. But if I do hear about it, I know who to send her after now. I'll see you at four o'clock." Selma let out a foxish grin and stalked out of the tavern, toying with the dagger at her hip.

Jonathon shivered, shaking his head. "Selma will be the death of me." He ate the last of his food too and got up, waiting for Jethro.

Jethro pushed away his plate too and stood. "Careful, don't say that too loud around a certain dragon. He may think you're serious." Jonathon shocked his head and laughed at the thought. He would have loved for Selma and Thermaxas to meet- he wondered if Selma would be as cocky as her normal self, or if she would let the dragon intimidate her.

"Well, it's a good thing said dragon is preoccupied." Jonathon waved away the thoughts that came to mind- of the evil that threatened Tarlatan. "Now, let's get to those children, before they come terrorizing the tavern." Jonathon placed his hands on Jethro's shoulders and pushed the man out the tavern, throwing gold coins on the table for the waitresses.

As Jethro and Jonathon walked to the apartment, he ran through the thoughts in his head. He knew the story better than any other. The story was his life… How could he not know it well? But going through it, remembering all those things, it was painful.

There were some things that he would have liked to remain forgotten. But these children needed to see what his destiny required, so that perhaps they might be prepared for their own.

Jonathon only hoped their own destiny had not required as much pain as his own.

The town of Clearford was still waking up. They had gotten up earlier to explore more of the city before Jonathon had to meet the children. The sun had risen and boats were beginning to pull out of the harbor. It was almost busier now than at mid day- ships who had stopped for the night market were looking to move onto the next port town as soon as possible. Other ships were starting voyages and some were new merchants, ready to start their adventure.

The windows were being thrown open around them, with ropes being pulled along as clothing got clipped to them. They were strung out to dry in the hot mid afternoon sun, but for now, dripped onto the people below. Jonathon wiped the water dripping from the clothes off his forehead and hoped the clothes would be dry on the walk back from the apartment.

Dogs roamed the street at this hour, not intimidated by the men and women rushing to the ports. They seemed to prefer this time of day, rummaging through the trash that had not been taken by other scavengers. Shop owners were just getting in, and didn't have time to shoo the dogs away.

"Do you think we're doing the right thing?" Jonathon asked, breaking the silence. Jethro glanced over at Jonathon, giving him a questioning look.

"I think… I think that it's worth looking into. I think it's the right thing for myself, and I'd even go as far as saying it's the right thing for you. At the end of the day, however, only you can say it's the right thing for you… Just like Selma, Jyn, and Namior are the only ones who can say if settling is right for them." Jethro explained, looking around at the buildings while they walked.

Jonathon sighed. "What if it isn't right for Selma, Jyn, and Namior? Will me and you settle and they leave?" Jonathon played with a loose thread on his sleeve. He didn't want to split up. He had been with this group for over half his life. Leaving them sounded almost as painful as leaving Thermaxas.

"I may not be able to say if settling is right for the three of them. What I *can* say is that I don't anticipate them moving around without me and you. We're a family. We're the only family we've all known for years now. I would never want to hold them back, and if they do leave and we stay here, that's okay too. But I think they'd want to try to create a life here before just leaving us." Jethro explained, calming Jonathon.

They explored around the city more before finally reaching the apartment. Jonathon and Jethro spotted the children sitting there, waiting eagerly. They each laughed, shaking their heads. Of course the children would make it there before the story tellers.

"Well, should I start with where I left off yesterday?" Jonathon asked, taking a swing of water to ready his throat. The children all eagerly said yes, awaiting their story. "Where to begin…

'THE SHELTER IN TRIFILLEM HAD PROVED TO BE PIVOTAL IN the aid of the women and children from Gruffenberg. It was found many of the children lacked a basic education, although they all spoke well enough. The mothers explained that the fathers had merely wanted their children to appear as well educated, so as to not catch the gaze of concerned travelers.

The staff at the shelter assured the mothers that it was normal for these sorts of situations. That the children would all attain an education, and the mothers who wished to receive one would be given the option after work.

All the mothers were given chores, after all. This shelter was unique in that any woman who went into the shelter was allowed to choose what interested them the most- library duty, kitchen duty, laundry duty, tutoring- they had the list given to them, and they chose. Each woman made a wage that was put into a bank account for her. The women could do what they chose with that money.

Jonathon and his mother had settled in nicely, taking the week to settle in before signing up for classes that interested them and getting chores.

Jonathon and his mother sat in a chair outside Prudence's office, waiting nervously for them to be called in. A mother and her three children walked out, all excitedly discussing their classes and chores.

"Momma, are you excited?" Jonathon whispered, huddling next to his mother. She rubbed his shoulders, kissing his forehead.

"I'm excited for new possibilities. We were kept from the world for so long- now we get to explore it." His mother whispered back, smiling at him.

A knock at the doorframe- Prudence was leaning out the door, waving at them. "Isabel, Jonathon, how nice to see you!

Are you ready to come on in?" Jonathon and his mother nodded, walking into the office.

It was a warm, welcoming office with the walls painted a light shade of green, with a tree mural to the left of the door. Huge windows filled the walls across from the door, looking out across the city of Trifillem. The corner to the left of the windows had toys strewn across the floor, with parchment and colored pencils thrown about.

In the direct middle was a round table with four chairs around it and behind the set was a desk with one chair. There were a few bookshelves around the room, full of scrolls and books.

"It should be a short meeting today, but I am available for whatever questions you may have. Isabel, would we like to start with your options?" Prudence questioned. Jonathon's mother nodded, brimming with excitement. She pulled out a list from her piles of paper and ran a finger down it. "Well, we have a few options for you. On your intake papers, you had noted experience with sewing, cooking, laundering, and gardening. We currently have needs with repairing clothing and laundering it, assisting the chefs, and harvesting the food while maintaining the gardens. Does any of that seem appealing to you, or did you have any other ideas?" Prudence read down the list, clicking her tongue at the end and setting down the paper.

Isabel furrowed her brows. "I was hoping to work with you, actually. I'd love to be able to help more women and reach out to businesses to assist the shelter. I know that I don't have much experience, but the past few months have made me realize that I don't want to just do housework." She looked at Prudence with a pleading glance. Jonathon hadn't seen such a look on his mother's face in a long, long time- the desperation of wanting something so badly, that she would beg if she had to.

"I was a woman in a similar situation to yours. When

Clarissa brought me in, I asked a similar question. I wanted to help the shelter, but I was desperate to explore the world around me." Prudence hummed to herself, thinking it over. "We would still need you to take on a chore inside the house, of course. Perhaps you can work in the garden, so that you're still outside." Prudence offered it lightly, placing her hand on his mothers.

Isabel smiled widely. "That sounds wonderful! It feels refreshing to be able to do good. Will I get a schedule?" She questioned. Jonathon looked up at his mother and-

His breath was taken away. He was young, he realized- but he had never seen so much hope and happiness in his mother's eyes. His father had destroyed all signs of hope and happiness the moment they sprouted.

The moment his mother stopped begging and relinquished her life was the moment he ran away to Thermaxas.

In truth, he hadn't known how he found Thermaxas. His mother had told him stories of the red dragon and his strength, ruthlessness, and power. When his father began...

When his father took all the life from his mother's eyes, something in Jonathon's soul had called out to him. It pulled him towards the mountains, as though a rope was pulling him closer and knotting so that it would not loosen.

Prudence grasped his mother's hand tightly. "That is wonderful! We will work out the schedule closer on Monday of next week, when your shifts begin. But you would likely begin at 7:30, when it is still cool enough to work in the gardens. You'd work in there for a few hours before you wash up, and meet me in my office."

Jonathon watched as she continued to go over the details of what she would need and what to expect. Prudence then turned to him, smiling gently.

"As for you, Jonathon... Children up until sixteen years old are required to go to classes. You won't have any chores, beyond helping your mother clean your and her room. You're expected to study in five subjects a day. We understand that you are still young, at only five years old. But they would be simple classes, enough to get you started. You will be taught by experienced tutors, as well as some of the woman who come through the shelter who have become tutors. Do you have something you're interested in?"

Jonathon thought to himself.

He had never been given a chance to be interested. His toys had been thrown out and the only thing he had been left with was his mother's stories.

"I like dragons..." He smiled to himself as he spoke, thinking of Thermaxas. Prudence nodded, writing it down.

"Well, we can certainly put you in a class where you learn about animals. You will have to take a class for reading and writing, as well as very basic mathematics. Perhaps we should also put you in a games class, where you can play with your friends? We also have a storytelling class, if you are interested." Prudence offered the classes, looking towards Jonathon and cocking her head.

"That sounds good. Will I be able to tell stories about Thermaxas?" Jonathon questioned, starting to smile more at the thought.

Prudence giggled, writing it all down before looking at him. "You can tell as many stories about Thermaxas as you would like. I'm sure our tutors would greatly enjoy it."

And so Jonathon and his mother lived, excelling at their tasks. Jonathon, as he grew more comfortable in the shelter, became more outspoken and confident in himself. His mother also grew more confident- she quickly became Prudence's assistant and soon coordinator. They remained within the shelter, focusing on building a savings.

Jonathon began to learn the shelter like the back of his hand as he grew. He found solace in the library, devouring book after book about myths and legends in between classes. As teachers offered short research classes, Jonathon eagerly accepted. Any excuse to learn about the history of the continent was taken.

But around him, the boys who were growing up along with him became rowdier. Some were just as well behaved as Jonathon, but others… Others were stereotypical young boys.

His mother, Isabel, became a representative for the shelter, and assisted new families that came in as they transitioned. His mother had grown more and more confident with each intake. The shelter was focusing their resources on women and children like the ones who had come from Gruffenberg. They had decided to take in the worst cases, where this shelter had been their only chance.

Something had felt wrong, though. Him and the other boys began to be avoided by other women, some just ignoring them. Jonathon was fine with that- if they were not comfortable talking to him, he would not press them. But those other boys that were not the same as him.. Jonathon had tried to tell them not to bother the women, but some would not listen to a boy younger than them.

By the time the boys were twelve, Clarissa pulled Jonathon and his mother into her office.

"We have a matter that needs to be discussed. As you are well aware, Jonathon and quite a few other boys have recently turned twelve or older." Clarissa started. Jonathon's mother smiled widely- he knew she was proud of him. Jonathon was excelling in his classes and was even being brought along on outreach missions to tell stories to younger children.

"He has been doing so well. The cooks absolutely love him- and he has begun a class where he has been doing a lot of research in the library. This has been an absolutely amazing opportunity!" His mother was pulling out papers of Jonathon's most recent work when Clarissa pushed them back.

"He has certainly been doing wonderful in his classes and the cooks appreciate his assistance. But issues, completely out of the boys control, have been coming up with other residents." Clarissa paused. "Isabel, you are well aware of the state that these women enter in. Some have a lot of healing to do. We have been focusing our efforts in homes that have been requiring a lot more assistance, and on women who were in situations far worse than our own. I am proud of the work we have been doing- but some of the boys have become rambunctious, as is normal for their age. And for some women... For some women, some of the behaviors these boys are exhibiting is triggering. I cannot just ask some to leave, and be seen as choosing favorites. If even one has to leave, then all above a certain age must leave."

Jonathon froze. His mother has said this was *their* new home. She never said they would have to leave.

His mother sputtered. "You told us they all could stay as long as they needed to. You said any woman and child would be welcomed. That the women could stay as long as their healing required, and the children could stay until they were eighteen. That even then, you would assist in finding homes. What is to happen with them now?"

Clarissa gave them both a look of pity- one that Jonathon wanted to wipe off her face. "The boys can still attend classes here, and will be allowed to do so until they are sixteen. From there, we will sponsor half of an apprenticeship of their choosing. In the meantime, I know several children's homes that will be able to take in the boys who have to leave. Any woman who would like to leave with her children is of course welcome to do so."

Jonathon's mother began to protest, began to pull the papers out again. He knew she wanted to show Clarissa how responsible her boy had been, and just how much he deserved to be here with her.

Now it was Jonathon's turn to push the papers back and speak. "Mother, it's okay. You have lived your life in fear and are finally free. You deserve to be here- you deserve to live your life." Even if his heart broke a tiny bit as he said it, Jonathon knew it was true.

He had found a dragon to save his mother. He would endure living without her if it meant her living her dream.

"Jonathon, I can find a place for us to li-" His mother started, but Jonathon cut her off.

"I know you pay a discounted price to live here. I've seen you try to find other apartments with no luck. I know how pricey the city can be... And I also know that this shelter has everything to offer you." Jonathon met her eyes. He watched the tear trail down her face, and felt Clarissa's eyes fall away from them.

Clarissa stood. "I'll give you two a moment." She got up from her desk and walked out of the room, gently closing the door behind her.

"Mother... I will be okay, I promise." Jonathon threw his arms around his mother, who gripped him tightly.

His mother took a deep breath, tears continuing to trail down her cheeks. "You are my brave, brave boy. I have no idea how you grew up so fast." Her voice was a whisper, as if lowering her voice could slow down time.

Jonathon pulled away from her, walking towards the door and meeting Clarissa outside. "Can you please give my mother the details of the nearest children's homes and have her bring it to our room when she is ready? I have to start packing."

And packing Jonathon did, trying to cram all of his things into three backs. He had gone from having nothing... And now he had so many things that he had no idea when, precisely, his life had become so comfortable.

He stuffed a few of his books, parchment rolls, quills, and ink bottles delicately into one bag. He was careful to wrap the ink bottles in old socks so that they did not break, and the quills were wrapped delicately. In another bag went his clothes and shoes, or as many of them as he could fit. In the last bag went his precious items- his stuffed bear, the quilt his mother made him, a drawing of Thermaxas, and a golden compass.

Even as he looked back, the room still felt like his own. Like Jonathon hadn't actually taken enough to even leave a dent- and that perhaps hurt more than leaving his mother.

It hurt more in the fact that he was leaving the first place he had found safe enough to call home after leaving Thermaxas. He would always have his mother, and would never truly leave her. But now Jonathon was leaving the first safe, secure, and stable home he had ever known.

Jonathon forced the grimace off his face and loaded two packs onto one shoulder and one on the other. He turned to look in the mirror and wondered the same as his mother...

How did I grow up so fast?

Jonathon knew the question was not worth dwelling on, so he turned back and walked down the hall. His mother had still not yet returned- so he went back to Clarissa's office, where he found her waiting outside. Clarissa stood beside his mother with the address of a children's shelter he could go to. Clarissa gave him a letter of endorsement, as well as a letter addressed to him. It finalized his school schedule, giving him specific times of the day to come in.

There was a note at the bottom of the letter-

I cannot offer every child this. Your mother has been instrumental in helping our shelter. Even you, Jonathon, have been instrumental in assisting the new children. In return for all the good you and your mother have provided, I will offer you work in the kitchens in between your classes as well as shortly after them. You will earn a small wage and we will still sponsor half your apprenticeship in addition to this.

Please know I cannot offer every boy who is leaving this opportunity. This is something that should be kept between us. Even if you must say you are going to the kitchens, please do not disclose that you are earning a wage.

- Clarissa

Jonathon pocketed the letter, nodding in appreciation to

Clarissa. Other boys were in the rooms with their mothers, many having a much tougher time than Jonathon and his mother did.

He supposed, though, that he did not blame the other boys and their mothers. It was a heartwrenching situation and, based off the look on Clarissa's face, one she did not like putting the women through.

Jonathon gave his mother one last hug before walking out of Clarissa's office into the street. Her office was the only one who had a door to the outside. She had claimed it was to easier to take clients this way.

Perhaps it was easier to dismiss heartbroken women and children this way, Jonathon cynically thought.

He trudged through the streets of Trifillem, the roads he had come to know so well. He avoided the sewage piles, knew which windows not to walk under at certain times.

Jonathon even knew which sections of the city to avoid. Trifillem, at large was a city for industry and apprenticing. It's city featured a small market and a port was for shipping items in and out of the city. Factories dotted the coast nearest the port and employed nearly half city alone. Since running those factories required a large administrative force, a large amount of the city was literate and educated.

He had considered a job in one of those factories at one point. He had considered it because of the good wages that were paid. It would have been enough on top of his mother's salary to afford an apartment in the city... But she was adamant that he focus on his studies.

Jonathon felt eyes on him, and as he looked around, he saw men closing in. He panicked, feeling fear enter his veins. He wasn't even in the worst part of town- he thought he had known well enough where to avoid.

The men forced him up against the wall, a knife at his throat.

"Well, well, well... What do we have here? City rat, eh?"

The man scoffed, his voice rough and his spit flying onto Jonathon's face. "Check the pockets. We'll look at the bags after we see what this rat has... He'll come with us after."

"I have a soul tie with Thermaxas the Bloody. You'll regret doing that." Jonathon threatened. He felt a flicker in his soul, as if questioning. Jonathon didn't know how to answer back, but did not try. He wanted to try to handle this.

Jonathon was frozen with the knife pressed harder against his throat, but felt courage rise up. Something in his soul told him to fight. He thought of Thermaxas. He thought of what the dragon would do, and Jonathon bared his teeth.

And- something came out of his mouth that Jonathon didn't quite know what to do with. Strange tongues flowed, a language that Jonathon had never heard. But it flowed from his soul, hissed like a roaring fire.

"We sure we want to go into his pockets?" One of the other men questioned, taking a step back. "He's speakin' strange tongues, boss."

The man holding the throat to Jonathon's throat was not scared, though, and before the man could, Jonathon shoved his own hand into his pants pocket and pulled out a gold coin.

This time it was not pure fear that ran through Jonathon's veins but thrill. He knew what the man would find.

The man laughed loudly as he saw the flash of gold, not quite looking closely at it as he shook his head. "That's all you got la-"

The man tried to swipe the coin, but halted when he got close. One half of the coin was pressed with the markings of a dragon scale, as if it had been squashed.

"I wouldn't take that if I was you." Jonathon hissed, speaking in the tongue of man this time. The knife fell from his throat, clanging to the ground. "I've already mentioned I have a soul tie with Thermaxas the Bloody. If you take me or this gold, he will hunt you down until you are nothing but a bloody pulp wishing he would kill you. And I will gladly watch." Jonathon hissed, taking strange delight in the men stepping back. A part of his soul he had never felt before was awakened.

"Listen, we don't want no trouble-" The man who had held the knife was cut off by one of his men.

"Please, we'll take off now- just don't tell Thermaxas..." The man who had spoken earlier, who had been threatened by the strange tongues, begged to be able to leave.

Jonathon had no hold on them. They could have left at any time and yet... They would rather have begged than run. The men went as far as getting onto their knees.

Jonathon pocketed the coin, before kneeling and looking in their eyes. "*Run.*" He hissed out, watching as they ran away.

Other people had gathered, watching both with fear and interest.

One woman dared question him. "How's a boy like you get so vicious? You didn't need to make those men beg, boy."

Jonathon adjusted the packs on his shoulders, patting the coin in his pocket to make sure it was safe. As he turned from the crowd, he turned his back on his life as he had known it. "Destiny is not for the weak."

❧

JONATHON GULPED DOWN THE REMAINDER OF HIS WATER AND belched loudly. The children giggled, running away as the story finished. One child- Remus- stayed behind, looking at Jonathon with a strange expression on his face.

"What..." The child's eyebrows furrowed as he fumbled for the word. "Tongue, did you speak?" He questioned, not letting his eyes move from Jonathon's lips, as though that same strange tongue would be spoken before him.

Jonathon laughed a little. "I was speaking the tongue of dragons. I did not know it at the time- it was not until I had met Thermaxas years later that it was revealed I could speak the tongue of the dragons. Even today, I can only speak it when I am truly scared, and channel that part of my soul." Jonathon paused. "I do not call upon that part of my soul often. The part of my soul that I share with Thermaxas scares me. I love Thermaxas dearly, but the person I became… It has saved me, but it is not someone I wish to be all the time."

The boy nodded, seemingly satisfied with the answer as he got up and ran off. Jonathon still sat there with Jethro, running through his memories.

He never liked to remember the person he had become. As if the moment he had spoken the tongue of dragons, his soul had pulled upon Thermaxas.

"You've never told me you speak the tongue of dragons." Jethro muttered, drinking his ale.

Jonathon was silent for a good moment before speaking. "That moment is not something I like thinking of often. And besides- I have never been able to speak it since."

Jethro nodded, thumbing the edge of his mug. "Have you ever seen that side of Thermaxas?"

"No. He has not shown me that side- but I have seen the aftermath. As have all of you." Jonathon remembered finding Gruffenberg. Even years later, life had avoided it. As if all life, even plants, knew that touching a dragon's gold was a death sentence.

Jethro and Jonathon sat there for a long while, not daring to speak. They watched passersby, waiting for the rest of their group and the owner of the residence. Selma was the first to join them on the bench, sighing.

"I'm not admitting that you two were right, but Clearford is rather nice." Selma huffed, crossing her arms.

Jonathon snickered. "Have a good time with Yvette?" He questioned, leaning back.

Selma snorted and shoved him. "She won't be hunting you down for her stool. She said she got it back- and yes, by the way, I did have a good time." Selma paused. "Do you think Jyn and Namior will come?"

"I think they have to show up. They'll be too nervous that there's a possibility we'd end up splitting up to *not* show today. I'm glad you're making friends, Selma. Another fox?" Jethro grinned, shaking his head.

"Yes, she is rather sly." Selma hissed, smiling just a touch.

Jonathon wondered if his destiny had been completed. Wondered if moments like this might last forever.

Jyn and Namior walked up, strutting in front of them and gazing up at the building. "Brother, have we built anything this big?" Jyn pondered. Jonathon could see the gears turning in Jyn's head and his eyes taking in as much of the foundation as he could.

"No, I don't believe we have. Perhaps if this doesn't work out, we could just build a house for the group?" Namior suggested.

"So, I take it you've come around to the idea of settling down in Clearford?" Jonathon asked slowly, getting up to stand before the brothers.

The two brothers shared glances before looking back at Jonathon. "Perhaps you were right. Perhaps it is time to settle down. It has been a while since our group was in Clearford, and I forgot the possibilities that were here. We would be fools to not consider settling here." Namior walked closer to Jonathon, stretching out his hand. "Jyn and I have no one else but this family we have created. If one wants to settle, Jyn and I will consider it too."

Jonathon grasped Namior's hand tightly and pulled him into a hug. "You and Jyn have become the best brothers I could have ever asked for. If settling is not meant for us, I understand. But... I appreciate you all considering it." He looked at everyone in his family. Jyn, Namior, Selma, and Jethro. A rag tag group that had ventured across the entire continent for over thirty years.

"Jethro told us of what happened to Thermaxas. He told us about the letter… Whatever you need of us, Jonathon, we will follow you and Jethro." Selma stood too, walking over to Jonathon. He glanced back to Jethro, who had a strange expression on his face. A mix of sadness and reminiscence, perhaps.

A man walked up towards the group, clapping his hands. "Well, it seems the potential buyers are all here?" Their group nodded, huddling together. "Why don't I get you all inside?"

And so, the next step of the group's journey began.

CHAPTER 4

APPRENTICE OR ADVENTURE

The apartment in the heart of Clearford had left the group reeling. It was a miracle it had not been taken yet. The price, however, was much more than Jonathon and Jethro could have ever expected.

He wasn't sure what image they gave off, but opulent and full of riches was not one of them. So Jethro, the owner, and Jonathon negotiated back and forth for hours before they decided to head back to the tavern.

Negotiations were far from over, but they felt unsuccessful. Jethro told Jonathon not to give up hope yet. They still had time to get this worked out.

So they had returned back to the tavern, all their hopes too dashed to think of food or alcohol. It was strange- the moment they had walked into that building, it was as if they had seen their lives laid out in front of them. And for being initially against the idea, Selma, Jyn, and Namior were almost taking it harder than Jonathon and Jethro.

The next morning was equally quiet, with the group not daring to speak at breakfast. Jonathon began to wonder if there was something more going on than just the building.

Perhaps it had something to do with the strange expression on Jethro's face yesterday.

Jonathon decided that he couldn't take the silence, and pushed the bowl away. He couldn't take it. As he was leaving, he heard them begin to speak in hushed tones before Jethro too pushed up from his chair and stalked back to his room.

Jonathon rushed into the street, his heart pounding in his ears. Something was wrong- they were keeping something from him. He walked down the Main Street, heading straight for the ports. He hadn't gotten up as early as he had the past couple of days, and in doing so, the port had already filled up. Boats covered the coast line, with some even moored away from the port as their sailors rowed in.

There was a bench at the port, where Jonathon took his seat. He could barely see the ocean that stretched out, all the way past the known lands. Ships covered the view, with sailors and merchants buzzing around the port. He thought of the Sentinel who had walked down the same street he had to get to this port.

He wondered if Thermaxas had beaten her to the Ionian Mountains, or if he had gotten there after her. Jonathon would have loved to see that encounter. Perhaps... Perhaps Jonathon should have gone with Thermaxas. Just to make sure he was safe.

Jonathon wondered where they would have gone, and where their adventures would have taken them. Maybe they could have discovered what was out west. Maybe they could have east to the Fae Kingdoms with the Sentinels and sought out help from the Fae Queen.

It would have made a beautiful legend, years down the line. The Queen of Darkness, the Queen of Starlight, and the Queen of Faeries all united as one to defend the world against evil.

Jonathon wondered if he had been through enough adventure in his lifetime. It had been a decision he made a long time ago. He could have chosen to continue his apprenticeship under a blacksmith, and make good money in Clearford.

Instead he had chosen a life of adventure, believing he could better help people by going on the road instead of staying as an apprentice. He knew they had made a difference. Him, Selma, Jyn, Namior, Jethro... They had all made a difference in someone's life.

But was it enough?

That gods damned Sentinel. Making me question everything, Jonathon thought miserably.

Someone sat next to him- Selma.

"What do you want? Or are you just going to sit in silence until I decide to leave?" Jonathon muttered. Selma sighed next to him, staring straight forward.

"You chose the best spot. Wonderful view really." Selma muttered back, crossing her arms across her chest. "We didn't mean to leave you out, but what needs to be said is something only Jethro can tell you."

"Thought so." Jonathon mumbled. Selma pushed him a little, shaking her head.

"Jethro will tell you when he's ready. Are you going to sit here and mope all day, or are you going to get back to the children to tell them another story?" Selma asked. Jonathon whipped his head up and stared in confusion at Selma.

"Stories? They want more?" Jonathon questioned. His brows furrowed. His life after meeting Thermaxas hadn't been that exciting- and the prospect of adventure wasn't with magical creatures or immortals, either.

"I guess so. They kept interrupting my walk over here to ask where you were. I told them you were on your way to satiate them, but the children are fickle beasts. They complained that you had just gotten to the good part yesterday, and you *have* to finish your story." Selma droned, rolling her eyes.

Jonathon and Selma stood together, but before they walked away, Jonathon grabbed her wrist. "I can deal with Jethro not telling me. But what I can't deal with is feeling like you are all talking behind my back." Jonathon explained. He had felt betrayed- Jethro should have told them all together.

But Jonathon wouldn't hold his anger against Selma, Jyn, or Namior. It wasn't their fault.

"Come on. Are you going to join me today? Jethro typically joins me, but perhaps the children might like a change of pace." Jonathon grinned, letting go of Selma's wrist.

"How could I miss out on the entertainment?" Selma grinned wickedly, joining Jonathon on the walk to the apartment. The further they walked from the port, the more Jonathon let go of his anger and frustration.

He could be patient.

By the time they got to the children, Remus was standing and tapping his foot impatiently. The children stood behind them, as if he was their ringleader and they were simply waiting for Remus to leave.

"Only a few moments late, and you're about to riot?" Jonathon laughed at Remus turning in shock.

"They look rather frustrated. Jonathon, maybe we should leave..." Selma shook her head, both her and Jonathon watching in earnest as the children's expressions changed from frustration to surprise.

Remus ran up to Jonathon and grabbed his hand, pulling him over to the seat. "No, no, no... We'll listen, you don't have to leave!"

Jonathon chuckled. "I suppose we should get back to my story. We shall begin where we left off..."

๏๙๖๑

'JONATHON SLAMMED THE HAMMER DOWN ONTO THE RED HOT metal. It was midday, but the blacksmith shop was lit only by the small fire in the forge and the lanterns along the stone wall. Jonathon did not mind the darkness, however. His eyes had quickly adjusted, and it allowed him to better see the glow of the metal.

Tools lined the wall, some purchased, some made, and some traded. Anvils dotted the space, ranging from hundreds of years old to made within the past ten years.

The floors were made of dirt, as the shop was not the finest in Clearford. It was a newly opened blacksmith shop, and the master could not afford the beautiful pumpkin wood floors that adored other blacksmith shops in the city. The walls were made of granite and the roof tiled with slate, so as to reduce the risk of fire. So many blacksmith shops had burnt down, before the masters who built them decided to invest more money into their shops so they might last longer. Light peeked in through the tiny holes in the stone, spaced just enough so that the room may have a little better ventilation.

"Jonathon, how's that order coming along? I've got the buyer coming in at the end of the day to pick up his horse-shoes and nails." The master blacksmith, Mac, shouted over the hammering. He pulled down on the handle that controlled the bellows, letting it breath air onto the fire so it might not die. "The iron monger is bringing a large shipment in shortly. There is steel coming from the Ionian Mountains, and iron is coming from the bogs in Oakgrove."

Jonathon nodded, pausing his hammering. "I'll keep an eye out through my window over here, and shout when I notice the shipment, sir. I'm on the sixth horseshoe. I just have two more to make, and then I can start on the box of 15 nails he requested. Do we have a coal shipment coming in anytime soon? We're beginning to run low, I've noticed." He hammered one last time before thrusting the shoe back into the forge, and pulled down on the bellows handle.

"Coal will be in by the end of the week. I believe we got a good deal with this shipment- it was sourced from the rock mines in Statium. This can be shipped over seas, and we're cutting out a great deal of cost to transport it over land from Westcourt." Mac yelled. His hearing had been damaged from the years and years of blacksmithing. The constant hammering, yelling to each other... It had degraded Mac's hearing. Yelling was now the normal tone, and Jonathon found himself having to remind himself that to everyone else, *yelling was not normal.*

Jonathon pulled the horseshoe out of the fire, noting the red glow of the metal that meant it was pliable to shape into the needed form. He placed it on the anvil, tweaking and hammering away until he was satisfied with the shape.

"Jonathon, can you hand me my new gloves? I just wore through my old ones." Mac called from the corner. He was working on tools and housewares, requiring more patience and experience.

Jonathon grabbed Mac's new dark leather gloves, which nearly matched his dark skin. He exchanged them for the old, worn through gloves which were nearly falling apart in his hands.

He returned to his anvil and kept working away, wiping the sweat from his brow. This order had been placed last minute, by a traveller who had miscounted on his original order that had been placed much earlier in the year. Now they were ready to set off on their journey, and needed the supplies as soon as possible.

They would be traveling for months at a time, and would go for weeks before reaching a town. Therefore, they would need supplies to shoe horses as needed and create temporary structures should the weather turn on them.

Today would not be a day that he took a break. Under normal circumstances, Mac made sure Jonathon ate lunch, and dinner on the days they ran late. But today, between the last minute order and shipments coming in... That would not be a guarantee.

Jonathon didn't necessarily mind it. He had been working with Mac as an apprentice since he was fifteen. Jonathon had convinced the women's shelter, since he had progressed so greatly in his classes, to let him start the apprenticeship early. Mac was glad to take Jonathon on as an apprentice.

His shop had become so busy and Mac desperately need the help. Mac had started giving Jonathon simple projects this year. Nails, hooks, horseshoes, door hardware… Nothing too complicated, and things that Jonathon could easily handle on his own.

So Jonathon and Mac worked hard that day, trying to finish up orders. The only break they took was to sort out the iron and steel, and before they knew it, the sky was darkening. Jonathon finished the last nail, getting the traveller's order put together in a box.

A knock sounded at the door, and Mac rushed to open it.

The traveller walked in, shaking Mac's hand. Jonathon was startled by his silver grey eyes, seeming to shine beneath the hooded cloak. The hood was pushed off, revealing dark brown hair pulled into a ponytail. His tanned, olive skin was marred by scars on his jaw and hands.

"Thank you, Mac. It's always a pleasure doing business with you. Here's a little extra for rushing for me. I'd rather not be stuck on the road without enough supplies." The traveller handed Mac a small pouch, and from the way Mac weighed it in his hand, Jonathon could tell the traveller had greatly overpaid.

"Jethro, we've been friends for years. I can't accept this much. You and I both know what those shoes and nails are worth." Mac tried to give the bag back to Jethro, but Jethro pushed it back into Mac's hand.

"Please, my friend. You've always done such great work." Jethro bowed his head a little, and turned to Jonathon. "Well, you've been doing great work too, I hear. Mac can't stop talking about how much you've been helping him out." Jethro shook Jonathon's hand, and inspected the horseshoes.

"Thank you, sir. I hope they work well for you on the roads." Jonathon bowed his head at Jethro, handing him the bag that contained the rest of the shoes and the box of nails. Jethro placed the shoe in the bag and pulled it shut.

He waved his hand at Jonathon, shaking his head. "No need to call me Sir. You can call me Jethro- I've known Mac here for nearly 20 years. We entered a blacksmith apprenticeship together before I finished up at 21, and joined a traveller's guild."

Mac wagged his finger. "No, you're leaving out the bit where the master blacksmith was so happy to get rid of you he practically paid to release you... Because you burned through his coal at double the rate of the rest of the apprentices!"

Jethro barked out a laugh and grinned. "Don't listen to him, lad. What's your name, you must be... sixteen, seventeen years old? And Mac here already has you doing all this work?"

"I'm eighteen years old. My name is Jonathon... It's just simple work for now, but I enjoy it. It keeps me busy." Jonathon smiled, bowing his head a little before turning around and taking his gloves. He began shutting down the shop, while Mac and Jethro took a seat and talked.

Jonathon was methodical, making sure the coals were spread out enough that the fire would go out quickly as he worked. Tools were organized, windows were wiped down, and the tables cleared. It would always be sooty, and he would never dare eat off the floor but even just doing these little tasks at night made the quarterly cleaning much easier.

"I'm off for the night, Mac. I'll see you tomorrow, at the same time?" Jonathon waved to the two men, about to walk out the door before Jethro shouted for him.

"Wait! Jonathon, stop for a moment." Jethro called, standing quickly. Mac tilted his head in confusion and Jonathon furrowed his brows.

"Is something wrong with the quality, Jethro?" Mac asked, his hand out for the disputed product.

Jethro shook his head, pulling his bag closer to him. "Jonathon, you remind me of how I was when I was younger. We're looking for one last man for the traveller's guild, and were planning to find him along the way... But you may just be the man for the job." Jonathon reeled back in shock. That was... Not what Jonathon had been expecting.

Mac sputtered, pulling his hand back quickly. "You can't just steal my apprentice! And he's nothing like you- he doesn't burn through all of my coal!" Mac shook his head. "Absolutely not."

"Should the boy want to join, I'd be happy to pay for him to leave his apprenticeship. It would be ample funds to find another apprentice or journeyman, even. That way you are not restricted to only those who could pay to enter into an apprenticeship."

Jonathon watched Jethro and Mac turn to look at him. Mac... Looked disappointed, and shocked, that his friend would propose such an idea. Jethro looked excited, but reigned in. As if the most exciting part was not yet even taking place.

"I... I don't know what to say. Where will you even go?" Jonathon sputtered, looking down at his hands. "When do I have to make my decision by?" Jonathon asked, not daring to look at Mac this time. He couldn't bear to see the disappointment that would have struck a lance in his heart.

"My traveller's guild is setting off tomorrow morning for a town in Statium. It's in need of drastic repair, and the schools are lacking. When we sent out word to towns and cities that we were looking to help rebuild them, Illium in Statium was the first to respond. You'd need to decide now. We need to leave tomorrow morning at dawn, and I need to make a payment now if I am to release you from your apprenticeship properly. I don't want to leave Mac here without the availability to find another apprentice quickly." Jethro explained. A bit of excitement fell off his face but hope remained.

Jonathon bit his lip, still not daring to look at Mac. Instead he looked at the forge, coals just barely glowing. They were almost completely in the dark, the blacksmith shop only lit by two lanterns.

He could see the road ahead, forked. One road was an apprenticeship, leading to stability. Guaranteed money, as long as he continued working hard. Perhaps as Mac grew older, the shop would go to Jonathon. It was a straight road, with only a couple twists and turns. The other road was adventure, with so many hills and sweeping paths that Jonathon couldn't see to the end. He could see that there was always a place for him in Clearford… But he did not have a permanent home. Not one that he could see, at least.

Jonathon stared down each path, seeing a future for him down both. Neither was dark or stormy.

"I'd like to go with Jethro." Jonathon spoke quietly, trying to ignore the swear that Mac let loose before sighing.

"Look at me, Jonathon." Mac took a step towards Jonathon. Against his soul yelling at him not to, Jonathon looked up. Mac's brown eyes had tears welling up, but there was no anger on his face. Not when he looked at Jonathon. "I've seen you grow up so much in your years here. I'll miss you, and I can't say I'm not mad at Jethro for taking one of the best apprentice's I've ever had… But if this is what you feel is best, you should go." Mac smiled, taking Jonathon's hand and shaking it.

Jethro set down the shoes and nails, pulling a pack off from underneath the cloak. In it was a large pouch of coins.

"I believe this should suffice. I've had it saved for a rainy day, and I can't think of a better time to use it." Jethro smiled, shouldering his pack again and picking up the bag of shoes and nails. "I am truly sorry to take Jonathon from you." Mac took the bag of coins from Jethro, and shook his head.

"It is fine, my friend. I cannot say that I'm pleased, but you're not leaving me empty handed." Mac smiled, and waved Jonathon and Jethro off. They left the shop, walking down the road together.

"I'm glad you said yes. There is one other person in the group your age- her name is Selma. She's recently finished all of the schooling her town can offer, and has traveled with the group to Clearford. She's a new recruit to the Traveller's Guild. There is a certain structure to this group. There are five top positions, and then contractors who work beneath the five top positions. Selma leads the teachers, as she has the widest education out of all of us. The other two are Jyn and Namior- they lead the builders, as they've got a sixth sense when it comes to building that I can't explain. I lead all the priests and farmers. And you... You are our assistant, bouncing between the four of us until you find what interests you. When you find an area you want to lead in, you let us know and we'll work with you on that." Jethro explained, moving his hands to and fro as he talked.

The pair continued walking down the road, heading towards the main town. The blacksmith was located just outside the main bulk of the city. Jonathon stayed on the edge, where it was close enough to be near the life of the city but not too far from the shop.

If only his mother could have heard about this.

How will she find out? Jonathon thought, the idea of his mother trying to contact him and not being able to find him running through his mind.

"When and where shall I meet the group? Besides the main five positions, how many other people are in the Traveller's Guild?" Jonathon asked, looking over at Jethro.

"Well, first it is important to understand there is a greater guild. My guild is merely a small part of the greater one- it is composed of nearly fifty people, not including the main five positions. The greater guild... Has nearly five hundred recruits, all spread across smaller guilds." Jethro paused. "You can meet us at the Powder Hollow Tavern at dawn. It's not too far from the main gates of Clearford."

Jonathon and Jethro paused, reaching the turn off to Jonathon's street.

"I'm glad I chose adventure." Jonathon spoke, taking one last glance at Jethro before striding off towards his apartment, with a smile on his face.

THE NEXT MORNING WAS FULL OF GREETINGS, EXCITEMENT, and last minute travel jitters. Some were worried they'd forgotten something, others worried they had taken too much.

Jonathon felt those jitters too... But a part of him felt as though he was returning to a long lost friend. Life on the road as a child had never been glamorous, but after the horrors of Gruffenberg, it was the most free he had ever felt as a child. He had dropped off a letter with a messenger on the way here, hoping it would reach his mother. He told her to direct any mail towards Illium, so that it might be there waiting for him when he arrived.

A woman strode towards him, the same age as him. The woman was short, yet lithe and light on her feet. She had strawberry blonde hair, with tan skin and golden eyes. A white streak of hair fell across the side of her face, blunt against the strawberry. She held out her hand, Jonathon shaking it.

"Jonathon?" She asked. He nodded, smiling. "Selma. Wonderful to meet you- I was surprised when Jethro told me we had found our fifth before even starting the journey." Selma mused, looking him up and down.

It was something that made him do a double take- her foxlike stare, the charm to her voice. It all made his heart thunder.

The charm though... He had seen it before, in the members of the Thieve's Den in Clearford. They were known throughout all of Western Tarlatan for their cunning, intelligence, and thieving skills. They bartered for secrets and traded in blackmail. Jonathon would have to keep his gold close and his thoughts closer.

"Ah, found me out already?" Selma purred, going arm in arm with Jonathon. He adjusted his pack, moving it to the other side of his body. "Don't worry, my skills are at bay. Jethro runs a respectable traveller's guild- I only plan on returning to the Thieve's Den when the guild splits." She let go of him as they approached Jethro and two other men.

Both certainly seemed older than Jonathon, but couldn't have been older than Jethro. Perhaps... Twenty five at most.

The men could have been twins. They featured the same golden blond hair, chocolate brown eyes, and tanned skin. They were tall and muscled, with calloused hands that had dirt permanently ingrained in them.

"Jonathon, so glad you made it in time. Meet Jyn and Namior. We're heading out in the hour, so excuse my short introduction. I have to get everyone organized. Can you three assist Jonathon with finding a horse?" Jethro bowed his head, giving Jonathon a smile that asked him to forgive him. There wasn't anything to forgive, but Jonathon did anyways.

And off they set before the hour was up, their guild of 55 traveling through the wilderness. For the most part they stuck to the road, Jethro unwilling to take a more scenic route despite the pleas of some of the teachers in the group. They had wanted to collect specimens on the way to the first town, the teachers said.

Jethro compromised that they could stop earlier than planned at nightfall so the teachers may still have daylight to collect specimens.

Day by day passed, stories being told around campfires. The jitters eventually left, and the group began to form a bond. The priests told the myths of their gods. One spoke of the falling of Makani, the god who loved humanity so much he used his breeze to ward the other gods away. Another told the story of the wrath of Alesia, whose tears turned the seas to brine after her mother died.

One day, however, the road turned more familiar than Jonathon could have ever imagined. Suddenly he was five years old again, running as far as he could, towards something that was calling for him.

Gruffenberg.

The group murmured ahead, seeing a glimmering in the distance.

Jonathon's horse paused as it felt Jonathon go deathly still.

Jethro turned, calling for him. Only instinct made Jonathon instruct his horse to continue forward.

The town indeed glimmered, gold covering it. The pathways were covered with it. The town square was simply a mountain of gold, a boat hull charred sticking out of it. Skeletons were strewn around, the gold a husk of where a body used to lay. The clothing stuck to the gold, tatters of it hanging.

It was a ghost town.

Jonathon couldn't breathe. His eyes dashed towards his old home, just outside the town square. The door had been pushed open as gold must have poured into the house.

He could see the burned remains of houses and taverns where the fire must have burned the hottest.

"We should leave here." The horses halted, but some men and women jumped off in curiousity.

"What is this place?" One asked.

Another replied, his voice grave. "A graveyard left by Thermaxas the Bloody. This place is cursed- we *must leave.*"

Jonathon would have echoed the sentiments, had he not known why Thermaxas had caused so much damage.

Someone stumbled upon a body, almost retching at the sight. "Look at what this monster did." Jonathon walked towards it, stumbling back in shock.

This was a corpse. As if it had died just moments before. A curse had been placed on it that only a dragon could have made.

"Legend says that only a black dragon could have left a curse on a body. The fire of the black dragon burns so hot, that a bit of the dark magic that created the dragon leeches out onto whatever it burns. But... I never knew the fire of a red dragon could burn so hot. I doubt this poor soul deserved it. Completely undefinable." One woman noted.

To most, the body would have been unrecognizable- undefinable. The corpse was blackened, limbs torn and hanging on by sinew. The head was rotated 180 degrees, facing outwards towards them. Claw marks laced down the back, with a hole where the heart would have been.

The spine had been ripped out. Whether it was ripped out before the heart was torn from the back, no one would have been able to tell.

Jonathon recognized the body, though. The scar that the fire burned permanently into the corpse, just above the right eyebrow.

One his mother had given his father, right before all hope had disappeared. It had been her last stand to protect Jonathon.

"That man was more a monster than Thermaxas would ever be." Jonathon spoke with more confidence than he thought he had in him at that moment.

A man scoffed. "No one deserves such torture. Dragons are mindless beasts. This town is forever cursed. Legend says that the women and children fled when Thermaxas rained molten gold upon it."

"No. Thermaxas rescued them- he was saving them. They were not here when the destruction happened. It was cursed far before Thermaxas covered it with his gold. Thermaxas had more of a soul than that man, with no heart or spine, ever did." Jonathon took a step back, eyes glued to the corpse. To the scar, that stared back at him.

"And how exactly do you know that?" A woman asked.

Jonathon wasn't sure if he wanted to answer that yet. None of these people knew who he was. If they thought Thermaxas was a monster... Maybe they wouldn't accept him in the group, if they knew he had a soul tie with a dragon.

But no one else asked Jonathon a question, nor did they expect an answer, and Jethro called for them. Jonathon noticed Jethro's weary eyes settle on him, even as he was warning the guild not to take any gold.

That thought rang through Jonathon's head, as he sat numbly on his horse.

That a fire had to burn so hot, it awakened a part of the dark magic that created the dragon. That only then could that dark magic leech and curse whatever it burned.

There were four colors of dragons. Black dragons were the deadliest, living in the tallest mountains and in the northern-most reaches of the world.

Red dragons were the second deadliest and roamed Tarla-tan, though most often stuck to themselves. So long as they had their gold, and no one tried to steal it, they most often left the world of men to themselves.

Blue dragons were the third deadliest, living amongst the islands of the sea. They did not dare roam Tarlatan, for fear of the red dragons. Instead they pillaged ships and hoarded their gold in sandy caves, sometimes spreading stories to the mainland to entice men to try and steal their plunder.

Gold dragons were the least deadly, but ruled over the four types of dragons. They were royalty. To be colored gold was to be almost a god. Even the black dragons bowed before the gold, despite having no care for nothing of the world around them. They protected the isle that the dragons lived on, which included the Fae Kingdoms.

It was an unspoken truce- the dark magic of the dragons

and the white magic of the Fae evenly matched the two. They would not attack one another, and would even attempt to protect one another.

Thermaxas had summoned a fire so hot, it rivaled a black dragon's fire. All to get revenge on the man that had caused Jonathon so much harm.

⚜

Jonathon stared out across the children, feeling a twinge of that numbness that plagued him that day seep in again.

As impatient as the children had been to get their story started, they were just as eager to go off and play. They ran off, following after Remus, disappearing into the streets.

He had never blamed Thermaxas for destroying Gruffenberg. No, he had been *happy* that town had been destroyed. The next day, once the shock had worn off, Jonathon had never been happier.

But despite that happiness, that free feeling of knowing his monster of a father was well and truly dead, the shock of seeing Gruffenberg still haunted him from time to time.

Selma stared at him in shock gulping. "I... I never realized that. Even when it was revealed that you had a soul tie with Thermaxas, I never thought much of it. Never thought back to Gruffenberg." She brushed that white streak of hair behind her ear and covered her mouth.

"It's okay, Selma. I try not to think of Gruffenberg too much anymore. I am glad for what Thermaxas did. But that day... Hearing them try to defend what my father had done... That may have been worse than seeing Gruffenberg again." Jonathon explained. A tear fell down his face. Jonathon didn't bother to wipe it. Selma had a tear fall down her face too- and she wrapped her arms around him, taking a deep breath.

"I wish I had known. Jethro may have ran a respectable

guild, but I would have shown them why the Thieve's Den is infamous that day to shut them up." Selma muttered, burying her face in Jonathon's neck. They had become close over the years, with Selma more a sister than anything.

Jonathon laughed, imagining eighteen year old, five foot Selma showing the men and women of their guild who exactly she was.

As the guild split over the years, with teachers, priests, builders, and farmers deciding it was time for them to retire, Jethro released them. Eventually it was just the five of them, and it had been that way for years now.

When Selma and Jonathon first met, he hadn't trusted her. But now... He trusted his life in her hands.

"As much as I appreciate the sentiment, I highly doubt we would have gotten this far if you had done that. But thank you, Selma. I appreciate you more than you know." Jonathon let go of her, taking a long sip of his water and closing his eyes.

Someone coughed in front of them- Jethro.

Selma excused herself hurriedly, dashing off to who knows where. Jonathon wished she hadn't been so quick, if only so he didn't have to be alone with Jethro. He wasn't angry with him, but hurt and disappointed. He wasn't sure if he was ready to talk with Jethro.

"I'm glad Selma knows. She and you became very close over the years. I'm impressed with how smart she is, that she never discovered the soul tie." Jethro spoke. Jonathon supposed Jethro might not know what to say either.

"It's easy to hide something in plain sight. If it's that obvious, people tend to overlook it, thinking it's too easy." Jonathon paused. "What's wrong, Jethro? Why won't you tell me what's going on?" Jonathon met Jethro's eyes, looking at the man who had become like a father to him. Those brown eyes were full of sadness.

Suddenly, it hit Jonathon like a ton of bricks how old Jethro had gotten.

Jethro glanced away, looking at the ground. Jonathon wondered if he always had those wrinkles.

"Do you want the good news or the bad news first?" Jethro asked.

Jonathon wasn't sure if he wanted to reply.

"Bad news." Jonathon muttered.

Jethro sighed. "I… There is a… growth on my ribcage. The healers can't tell what it is. It's not magical, not a curse… But certainly not normal. It's been wearing my body down more so than usual. I find myself more and more tired, my limbs aching more, and I *hurt*. The healers have seen this before. They estimate that if it spreads, I don't have much longer."

Jonathon dropped his water pouch.

"I got the building. I spent most of my time yesterday not negotiating, but getting my affairs in order just in case. The building is in your name entirely. All of my wealth, all of my belongings, the guild… It all goes to you. Selma, Jyn, and Namior know they are to follow you when I pass."

Jonathon stood abruptly. "No- no. I won't accept it. You can't die. Not now. We still need you." Tears flowed down his face. They fell down Jethro's, too. Jethro stood slowly, and placed a hand on the side of Jonathon's face.

"I'm not going yet, Jonathon. But when I do… It will be alright. I promise. It may hurt, but it will be alright. You haven't needed me for a long time." That sad smile returned to Jethro's face.

Jonathon closed his eyes, throwing his arms around Jethro.

He nodded in agreement with Jethro, but silently to himself, Jonathon pledged to find something to heal Jethro. He would not let him pass so easily.

CHAPTER 5

THE BURDEN OF FATE

F ate is a concept made out to be complicated. It is described as though one can avoid fate. That, there are so many complications, that fate has a blind spot in between all those complications.

Jonathon knew well, however, that fate had no blind spot. Fate did not have an eye to stab or ears to cover.

He should have known that if Jethro was doomed to die, fate would find a way to take him. But still, he pretended. Pretended as though nothing was wrong, and they all had an unlimited amount of time together.

All five of them pretended. Even when they were moving, Jethro pretended he was still as strong as he once was. Perhaps it wasn't smart, and perhaps they should have made Jethro rest, but... Jethro wouldn't have let them coddle him anyways.

It was a long day- after the discussion yesterday, Jonathon made the decision that they were to move in as quickly as possible. Given that they had lived on the road for the past nearly thirty years, the five of them didn't have too many belongings. It took them a day to completely unload the chests that were kept in the stables, and the packs that were kept in their rooms in the tavern.

Jyn and Namior even got the horses and their mule stabled closer to the building. Eventually they would rent their horses and mule out to a local farm in exchange for boarding the animals. Everything was seemingly going smoothly. Almost as if Jonathon had outrun fate. And for a moment...

He was tricked into thinking that just *maybe* he could escape fate this one time.

Jethro stumbled, showing the first signs of weakness Jonathon had seen him show since jumping off the horses upon their arrival into Clearford.

Jonathon rushed to his side, dropping the books in his hand.

"Are you okay?" Jonathon murmured, placing a gentle hand on Jethro's back to steady him. Jethro held a hand up, taking a deep breath. He stood there for a moment, before standing straighter and shaking Jonathon's hand off. "We can get you a healer to see if they can do anything for the weakness and-"

"Jonathon, there is nothing the healer can do for me. Only the gods can decide what happens to me now." Jethro interrupted Jonathon, looking down at him.

Jonathon shook his head. "No, there must be something they can do. Anything. Can they not remove the growth?" Jonathon wondered, his eyes glancing down towards Jethro's ribs.

"If they could remove it and stop the spread of whatever the growth is, I would have already had it done by now. But they believe the growth has spread far further than their powers can see. It is not safe." Jethro walked over to the couch, a small limp in his step, before taking a seat.

Jonathon wondered if that had always been there, and why he was just now noticing it.

"Would removing it not give you a chance?" Jonathon knelt before Jethro, looking up into his eyes. Pleading to try *anything.*

"If it has already spread..." Jethro paused, looking away. "Removing it would only delay the inevitable. I do not want it to be slow and painful. I do not want your last memory of me to be nothing but pain and suffering." Jethro whispered, closing his eyes.

I do not want your last memory of me to be nothing but pain and suffering. The words echoed in Jonathon's head. His soul ached, a fire building within.

Last. Memory.

A road appeared before Jonathon. If he looked back, there was that same windy road that he had chosen so long ago. And now, there was a straight path. A straight path towards darkness if Jethro died.

Except there was no other road to take, no other path that split off. This was Jethro's fate. Jonathon knew that darkness he saw was pain and grief. He knew it was likely there was light after it...

But the darkness plagued him, caused that fire to burn brighter as if he could try to burn it away.

"So that is it then? There is nothing to do except watch you die?" Jonathon snapped. Him and Jethro had been closer than family. The only ones Jonathon had ever been closer with was his mother and... Thermaxas.

Thermaxas, who he could not even feel. Who he could barely feel- the soul tie was there, and he could feel his fury. His confusion. His pain.

He was not sure why Jethro had just given up. They had travelled for so very long, that was for certain. But was there not a chance of finding a healer that could fix him? Was there not some long lost magic that they could find in history books to reverse fate?

That fury built, fury that Jonathon knew he had no right to direct at Jethro. But still it built...

And only just slightly, only enough that Jonathon was left even more on edge.

Jonathon shot up from his knees and paced in circles, trying to ignore Jethro's worried stare. "Jonathon?" Jethro whispered, standing slowly. It angered Jonathon, for some reason. Seeing the old man stand. And that anger…

Was anger he had not felt in such a long time.

Jonathon clutched his hands to his head, feeling the words flowing to his tongue. He bit down on it hard, but they did not stop. They hissed out of him, a dark fury that caused him to double over.

Jonathon barely noticed Jethro rush to his side, calling for Selma, Jyn, and Namior- wherever they were.

His head was splitting. It was so painful, and the soul tie was so strained. As if the knot was tying around his soul in a way it never had before.

A voice came through his head, as if it was so distant it might have been thousands of miles away.

Jonathon. Jonathon please, I don't have much time.

Thermaxas. It was Thermaxas-

Yes, yes it is boy. Please listen to me. I need you to go to the Fae Kingdoms and head to the very north of the Isle.

North of the Fae Kingdoms? But that was where-

Yes, that is where the dragons lay. Please, my boy. We need you. We need the dragons. This evil… It is a plague that will destroy us all and if they get to the dragons first…

We may never survive. Thermaxas didn't need to finish for Jonathon to know what he was about to say.

Run, boy. Sail with the dragons wings at your back. Go to the Ionian Mountains when you are finished.

Did the dragons know he was even coming?

No, boy. They do not. And if you call for me… I will not be able to answer. It is the reason you need to go, and I cannot. You are the only other one who can speak the tongue of dragons.

Please, Jonathon.

. . .

JONATHON SHOT UP, HIS HEART RACING. JETHRO SAT OVER HIM, Selma on one side while Jyn and Namior were on the other. They took a step back, letting Jonathon breathe for a moment. His soul scrambled, reaching out for Thermaxas. He pulled on the rope that connected his soul to Thermaxas' and tried to find the tie. It was there, and he could feel the rope that extended to Thermaxas.

But it was so strained and if he shouted for Thermaxas, he might have shouted into the void.

Tears streamed down on his face as he sat on the ground, his soul scrambling to find Thermaxas. Before, he could almost feel what Thermaxas was doing if he tried hard enough. Which was, most of the time, sleeping in a curled up ball waiting for thieves to try to steal his gold.

Now it was next to nothing, the only indication of the bond being that rope tied in the middle.

"Jonathon?" Jethro whispered, staring at Jonathon with concern.

Jethro. The memories flooded back to Jonathon, and the harsh words that had flooded out of his mouth before... Before Thermaxas had commanded a soul tie in a way that Jonathon had never felt before. Even when he had spoke the tongue of dragons to scare off the men in Trifillem, he had been in control.

Whatever had happened... Jonathon had not been in control.

"I'm so sorry." Jonathon let the words pour out of him, holding his still pounding head in his hands.

Jethro sat on the ground next to Jonathon and rubbed his back. "It's okay, Jonathon. Can you tell me what happened?"

What hadn't happened? Jonathon nodded though, despite the thought.

"Thermaxas... I... I can't feel him. I feel the soul tie, and can pull on it with all my might, but I can't feel *him.* He called for me and spoke to me- something we've never done. He

asked for me to sail to the Fae Kingdoms and go to the
northern part of the Isle and when I have finished there, I
must go to the Ionian Mountains." Jonathon didn't care that
Selma, Jyn, and Namior were there. They would find out
eventually, so he told it all.

"Did he say why he can't go?" Jethro titled his head,
furrowing his brows.

"This evil is far worse than Thermaxas expected. He must
go somewhere else and I am the only one who can speak the
tongue of dragons." Jonathon stopped for a moment before
looking at the three others. "Did Jethro explain... What is
going on?" Jonathon questioned, looking back towards Jethro.

"Yes, he did. It was a part of what he explained after
revealing his... Condition." Not even Selma could say it out
loud. Despite the fact they were facing world threatening evil
darkness that might just kill them all, no one could still say
that Jethro...

No, Jonathon would't go there. *Couldn't* go there.

"When do you leave?" Jyn asked, kneeling down.

Jonathon shot a surprised look at Jyn. "What makes you
think I'm going?"

Namior rolled his eyes. "The dragon just caused quite the
commotion to get the message across. I didn't realize you had
a choice." Namior raised an eyebrow as if it was the most
obvious thing in the world, and couldn't fathom that Jonathon
even thought he had a choice.

"I cannot get to the Fae Kingdoms on my own, let alone
venture into the northern part of the isles by myself. Perhaps
if Thermaxas could come, I would have a chance. But there is
no guarantee that the dragons would let me leave the Isles,
and if I do not get back to the Ionian Mountains..." Jonathon
didn't finish his sentence. He didn't want to think about how
the world might shudder before the might of Thermaxas the
Bloody.

Gruffenberg had become a barren land of gold and bone,

and Jonathon had survived. If Jonathon didn't survive the northern part of the Isles... Thermaxas would destroy the evil all on his own.

"You wouldn't be alone, Jonathon." Jethro smiled, and Jonathon wondered what might have made the man so happy. He supposed the confusion had spread to his face, because Jethro decided to explain it further. "The guild has been deeded over to you. The moment I found out that I might not have much longer left, I took care of the guild."

Selma, Jyn, and Namior knelt on one knee before Jonathon.

"We vowed to follow Jethro until the guild split. Now we vow to follow you, no matter the cost, and ensure that you make it to the Isles and back." Selma spoke confidently, the same charm in her voice that had been there when he first met her. And yet, he would trust her with his life now.

"Can you give me and Jonathon a moment?" Jethro whispered, moving to sit next to him. The three of them left the room, glancing back towards Jethro and Jonathon.

"I cannot make them risk their lives for me." Jonathon whispered. They were his family- if he lost them... He didn't know what he would do.

"You're not making them do anything, Jonathon. They did this of their own free will. The guild transferring from me to you broke their requirement to stay. They could have left at any time these few days and chose to stay. They believe in this." Jethro explained. Jonathon looked down at his hands.

"I suppose you're right." Jonathon's mind was whirling.

"You know far better than most that if their fate was not to go, then they would have left a long time ago. Fate is not predetermined, but instead choices that they would have made all long. No matter what the circumstances were, the three of them would have chosen to stay. If it was not a growth on my ribs, it would have been some other life threatening issue. It is not some other being that determines their fate- they choose it all on their own. It is simply a choice they would make the same decision for, time and time again. Fate knows this, and guides us all along our paths. We create the future, and fate ensures we follow the path we make." Jethro reassured Jonathon, both of them looking out the windows of the apartment. Being on the third floor, it overlooked the rest of the city and the ocean past the ships.

This city may have been one of the *least* peaceful cities they could have chosen to settle down. It was bustling day and night. No one was afraid of the darkness here. In fact, Clearford possibly thrived more at night than during the day.

It was ironic, considering the darkness and evil that threatened Tarlatan.

But it was not all dark. Clearford lit up the night, defying the darkness. Perhaps if Clearford could... The rest of the world could too.

Jonathon turned towards Jethro, the corners of his lips turning up. "Would you be okay if I ran the guild... A little less respectably than you?"

JONATHON CONVINCED SELMA TO BRING HIM, JYN, AND Namior to Yvette's without explaining a single part of his plan.

They were slightly concerned at his bought of confidence and energy, given the fact that he had been on the floor less than an hour ago. But Jonathon strode into Yvette's, noting the stool that was now chained to the bar.

Yvette stood behind it, polishing the mugs as she stared them down. Her store shelves were stocked to the brim, ready for the night market to open. Lanterns were freshly lit on the walls, and daggers were tightly strapped to her hips.

"Here to take my stool again? You'll have a little trouble with that. I noticed you didn't bother returning it, and I had to hunt it down myself." The words hissed out, only a little amusement behind them. Yvette rolled her eyes and put the mug and rag down.

Jonathon smiled, shaking his head. "No plans on taking any stools today. I have another proposition though. Jethro has deeded his guild over to me, and I'm starting an adventure… One that the Thieve's Den might be interested in." Jonathon explained. Selma looked at Jonathon in surprise, glancing over at Jyn and Namior. They merely shrugged their shoulders- they knew as little as she did.

Yvette smirked a little, reminding Jonathon that he was not dealing with a mere lackey. This was the leader of the Thieve's Den.

"Where are you going?" Yvette pondered. Before Jonathon could protest, and tell her it was secret until she agreed, Yvette continued on. "Any adventure that requires protection from the Thieve's Den, tells me that it's not your… Average adventure. I want in, and I want all of the details." Yvette pulled out a scroll, unrolling it and setting a mug atop it so it didn't roll back up. A quill was placed next to it, with the inkwell placed next to it.

"I require the Thieve's Den for more than just protection. This is more than a traveller's guild can handle. I need the cunning skills of the Thieve's Den, along with your other more… Physical, skills. There will be fights, and there will be killing. We'll be traveling through the Fae Kingdoms, and moving up through into the mountains. We'll need to venture to the northern part of the Isles, where the dragon's lay. After that, we'll need to ensure safe passage to the Ionian Mountains. I cannot guarantee everyone will make it out alive." dipped the quill into the inkwell, and filled out his name on the scroll. There he filled out the name of the guild, the leaders, and the main locations they would be adventuring to.

"I would expect nothing less from the man who engages with Sentinels and shares a soul tie with a dragon. You're an enigma, Jonathon." Yvette let the smirk fall. "The Thieve's

Den typically requires a cut of 25 percent of the total reward on top of the 500 silver requirement, but considering you're only promising us death as a reward, I'll let that part slide. 600 silver, and you've got a deal. How many men and women?" Yvette took the quill from Jonathon, dipping it again in the inkwell.

"I'd say fifteen of your finest, should do." Jonathon estimated, watching as she began writing.

She filled out her requirements and pricing, as well as the time she estimated it would take them. Six months, she wrote. Jonathon thought that was generous, but Yvette explained that sailing to the Fae Kingdoms would take up no small chunk of time. Then they would have to convince the Fae they were up to no nefarious deeds, and would have to survive the dragons. Only after that, could they even consider the amount of time it would take to sail back to the Ionian Mountains, and travel home to Clearford.

"Selma, I have a proposition for you." Yvette turned her gaze towards the woman, who brushed that white streak of hair behind her ear.

A blush appeared on her cheek and Jonathon almost did a double take. Selma, *blushing?* He would have to find out what exactly happened between Yvette and Selma.

"Yes, Yvette?" Selma asked, batting her eyelashes. Even the tone of her voice had changed. Yvette batted her eyebrows back, leaning on her elbows that were on the bar top.

Jonathon hoped that these two could at least wait until they were in their own tent.

"I'd like you to join the Thieve's Guild as my second. On a journey like this, I'd trust no other." Yvette looked towards Jonathon. "I understand she is likely vowed to your guild, and would gladly take the cost of that off of our fee to assist you."

Selma balked at the idea, her mouth agape. "I'm sorry Yvette, but I have been a part of this guild for the past thirty years. I can't just leave now." She blinked a couple times, staring Yvette in the eyes. Yvette didn't respond, just kept staring.

Jonathon turned to Selma, only glancing at the contract for a moment. "You told me all those years ago that the moment the guild split, you'd return to the Thieve's Den. This is your home, Selma. You cannot pass up the opportunity, and I couldn't imagine requiring you to pay to be released from your vow." He nodded his approval, although Selma had never needed it. If she had said yes without even consulting him, he still would have waived the payment.

Selma looked at him, squinting a little, as if she was waiting for him to change his mind before she eagerly turned to Yvette and nodded.

"I would gladly rejoin the Thieve's Den. I shall stay after Jonathon, Jyn, and Namior leave to draw up a contract with you and... Give my vow." Selma winked at the end, causing Jyn and Namior to roll their eyes.

Jonathon and Yvette finished out their contract, drawing up the rest of the details. They decided they would leave within the week, given the trouble that Thermaxas had gone through to get the message to Jonathon.

And with that, there was only one piece of business to take care of.

Jonathon spent the rest of the day traveling to Trifillem, hoping she had not moved.

In that same alley they ventured into, so many years ago, Jonathon approached the double doors and knocked.

A woman he had never met approached the door, opening it.

"Can I help you?" She gave him a skeptical look, and Jonathon supposed it was unusual for men to approach the shelter.

"My name is Jonathon, I'm looking for Isabel. Does she have a moment?" He averted his eyes, knowing some of the women were uncomfortable with direct eye contact. The woman furrowed her brows, but held up her hand before walking away.

He heard her whisper, despite her best efforts to keep quiet. "Isabel... There is a man here named Jonathon, wondering if you have a moment."

Not a second passed before a chair was heard being pushed loudly, scraping against hardwood flooring. Feet pounded towards the open door, and there was his mother.

His mother whom he had not seen in years. Her once jet black was now almost completely gray, but her blue eyes were still as piercing as ever. No matter how old she had become, Jonathon had never seen her more lively than she was now.

His mother smiled brightly, grinning from ear to ear. "My boy!" She threw her arms around him, breathing in deeply. "Please, come in, come in." She let go and pulled him into an office, just around the corner from the main doors.

"Is this your office, mother?" Jonathon asked as he looked around, inspecting all the knick knacks on the shelves and the flowers around the room.

His mother had never been allowed to have a personality and decorate when they lived in Gruffenberg. Over the years she had let her personality shine.

"Yes! Prudence retired just a few years ago, and I took over her position. They let me choose an office of my own. I wanted to be as close to the main entrance as possible, given I was going to be dealing with families that were just starting here. I hope you don't mind, I had taken some of the gadgets from your alchemy classes and some of the animal specimens. I found them incredibly fascinating, and wanted to be able to show families the possibilities there were for classes." His mother was still grinning as she took a seat in one armchair, and he sat next to her.

"I don't mind at all. I wasn't using them- I'm glad you got some use out of them. It looks wonderful in here... I'm so proud of you." Jonathon looked at his mother's face, taking it all in.

Her grin fell a little, as she inspected his face. "What's wrong? Why have you come today? You are always welcome... But something feels off." She frowned, and placed her hand on his own.

"I came to say goodbye, mother." Jonathon sighed, grabbing her hand and clutching it tightly. She closed her eyes for a moment, a tear running down her cheek. When her eyes opened, they were full of pity.

"Fate has not been kind to you, my dear." Her voice was quiet. It had grown crackly over the years, as if talking day in and day out had worn down her throat.

"I have made this decision by myself. If I do not go... This world may not last long." Jonathon sighed, looking away from his mother.

She sat up straight, and let go of his hand. His mother walked over to her desk, pausing to the right of it. She did not wait long before opening the drawer and pulling something out, hiding it behind her back. She walked back to him, taking a seat again.

"My dear, the burden of fate is heavy. It is unfairly heavy upon some compared to others." She pulled the object from behind her back, revealing a dagger. "I had stolen this from your father when you were only four. He was growing more violent as you grew older and more capable. I vowed that if he hurt you, I would use his own dagger against him. Eventually, I vowed that if we were not rescued from that awful situation, I would use it on the both of us. I want you to take this, and use it to keep you safe. I never had to use it, but I believe the gods saw my terror, the terror that caused me to vow something unthinkable. I would not let him do the things he had done to me on you."

She held out the dagger to him, still in its sheath. It was not a special blade by any means. It was common and cheap, but strong. The sheath itself was brown leather that was meticulously maintained.

"Mother, if I do not come back or write to you within a year... Go to the Ionian Mountains. It is the only place you will be safe, and I fear what will happen if I do not return." He spoke roughly, accepting the dagger.

"If you do not write, how do I know you have returned? Where are you even going?" Her question rang through his head, and there he was, staring down the path again.

"I must travel to the domain of the dragons. If I do not return... You will know by a roar that will be heard around the world."

ACKNOWLEDGMENTS

I'd like to take the time to thank all of you for the success of Origin of Exiles and the Fables of Tarlatan! I've loved writing since I was a child. Reading was my way of escaping... I could place myself into the mind of a character and forget about the problems around me. It was my greatest form of healing as well as my greatest form of learning. I hope that, in any of my books, the reader can find a character they have a bond with. Even if the reader cannot relate to specific struggles of a character, I want a reader to be able to relate to one of my characters.

Origin of Exiles has launched this entire world that I could have never expected to have created. It started with short stories I had written years ago- some being mere paragraphs long. Some were only dialogue. I have placed all these books under the full series *Fables of Tarlatan* so that the world is easily accessible. If it's a part of *Fables of Tarlatan*, it will have an affect on the overarching series and plot. Some will be side stories like this one that, while they have a plot, they'll be a way to world build more outside of the main books.

I'd never be able to do it without my fantastic editor, Jillian Rousseau, either! She's been an amazing help combing through my work and ensuring that I'm publishing my best work.

I'd like to thank everyone who has made this possible and supported me throughout this journey. I couldn't have done it without any of you!

ALSO BY SAMANTHA DEPERGOLA

Fables of Tarlatan Series
Book One: Origin of Exiles